I0594468

Queerly
ever after

Alayna Cole

MONRISE

Meanjin, Australia

Copyright © 2021 Alayna Cole

All rights reserved. No part of this book may be reprinted or reproduced or utilised in any form or by any electronic, mechanical, or other means, now known or hereafter invented, including photocopying and recording, or in any information storage or retrieval system, without permission in writing from the publisher.

ISBN 978-0-6453392-3-9 (Paperback)
ISBN 978-0-6453392-4-6 (eBook)

Cover artwork from Europeana
Cover design by Alexander Coolican
Typeset by Wallea Eaglehawk

First published in 2021

Revolutionary University Press is an initiative of Revolutionaries to publish the work of emerging and established creatives and thinkers from university places and spaces. One press for all universities.

Moonrise
Meanjin, Australia
www.moonrise.revolutionaries.com.au

Other titles from Moonrise

Madness in Bloom edited by Ross Watkins & Jay Ludowyke

a record of my remnants by Katie Hulme

Through the darkness, I will love myself edited by Wallea Eaglehawk, Nikola Champlin & Padya Paramita

Contents

Dedication

To anyone still trying to figure out who they are.
To Ross, who helped me find myself.

I

INNOCENCE

Once upon a time, in a land not unlike your own, someone drank from her tumbler of flaming whiskey and examined her dirt-smeared cheeks in the reflective glass. The crystalline surface depicted her streaked face near-perfectly, a trait the someone disliked about mirrors. She frowned at the tumbler—disappointed in both its reflective nature and its newfound emptiness—and cast it aside, where it danced hollow, thudding circles on the polished timber.

The someone abandoned the dysphoria forced upon her by her barren glass and returned to the distance of the darkroom. The safelight overhead droned like the out-of-tune lullabies her mother used to hum at her bedside. In its sunset glow, the someone processed photographs of skeletal trees reaching towards black skies from hazy hills of snow.

Overhead were rows of dried images, like windows into other worlds. Monochrome trees and houses were secured to the string by the grasp of wooden claws, and between these familiar images swayed a shadowy jawline. The someone recognised the semblance of a face she wished was not her own.

'What is this?' she asked.

I gave up my feigned interest in the enlarger I was hunched over and looked across the darkroom to the someone's shaking figure. 'It is a photograph of my love.'

'Then I do not need a love as ugly as yours,' she exclaimed, then fled the room, carrying the pungent fumes of developer and dysphoria out into the snow.

If I were you, I would now be forced to abandon this tale, as the someone's movements become hidden from my eyes by distance and debris, but contrary to the rules by which your world abides, I need not see the someone to know her story.

I did not always intend to remain in the darkroom, unpinning photographs from the overhead lines. At first, I considered chasing the moon alongside the someone, my ownerless footprints appearing in the snow. It took only a moment for me to think better of the impulse: she had always seen through my invisibility, and she would only grow more bitter if she knew I had not let her walk alone.

Regrettably, she was not as alone as the vision of her trudging through the snow suggested.

The Snow Queen's cloak left marks in the snow like a corpse being dragged between the trees. She shook her head at the someone's feet, which had become blotched with the colours of bruises and burns. She conjured a sleigh, and offered the someone a seat atop a pile of white fur. The someone had heard stories of the Snow Queen, her magnificence outweighed only by her indifference. Stepping onto the sleigh, the Snow Queen's laughter was as cold as the snowflakes that fell upon the someone's lips.

The sleigh carried the someone and the Snow Queen through parts of the forest I did not recognise, despite the many years that I had lived in this house among the trees. I wondered if the paths were conjured like the sleigh, and like the Snow Queen herself: magical figments leaking into our world from those that adjoin it.

An imposing shadow covered the sleigh as a building, with towers rising above the treetops, formed before the someone's eyes. The Snow Queen's sleigh rushed towards it and the someone realised only then that no animal helped to propel the vehicle, the reigns slack in the Snow Queen's hands. The sleigh halted before doors twice the someone's height, and three times as heavy.

Years ago, the someone's father took her to a cathedral to pray. Unable to hear within the minds of the others, the someone could replicate only what she saw, so she knelt in silence before the windows of coloured glass and thought of nothing. She entered a similar space now, the hem of the Snow Queen's cloak streaking the floor with slush.

The walls were adorned with tapestries, torn and faded. Portraits had been ripped from their frames in ribbons, leaving only the outlines of displaced limbs painted in oil. Places once filled with mosaics of coloured windows were shattered by the icy wind.

At the end of the aisle, where an altar might have stood, was a mirror larger than anybody—man or creature—that I had ever encountered. The Snow Queen guided the someone along the aisle to the base of the stairs that led to her reflection. Here she paused as the someone resisted, her patience waning.

'Stand before the mirror, child.'

The someone's feet remained affixed to the timber floor, as though frozen. Yet, although she did not move, the mirror came closer until the someone could see herself reflected there.

The reflection took my photograph of the someone and manipulated it, extending her jaw, widening her nose, setting her eyes deeper into a shrunken face. The image it projected was not the someone I knew, and yet the someone recognised herself within it.

The someone snatched a heavy candlestick from a nearby display of forgotten reverence and pitched it at her countenance, shattering the wicked mirror. A hundred million million and more pieces danced across the cathedral floor, finding corners and shadows in which to hide.

Some pieces were stolen by the icy wind and thrown into the sky. These found rain- soaked scenes to corrupt with the ugliness that the someone had seen within the looking- glass. The reflections eroded mountain ranges and stripped forests of their leaves, burnt the golden wheat fields and muddied the cobalt water of rushing rivers.

Some such fragments were large enough that they might be found and formed into window panes or spectacles through which the world could seem distorted and broken when looked through by those with weak hearts and cold eyes. Other shards were so small that they could be inhaled, lodging themselves within a person's throat and colouring their words with hidden hatred.

'Now, look what you have done,' the Snow Queen said.

'She did only as you knew she would,' I screamed, my words lost to the shadows of the darkroom and the white of the snow.

The Snow Queen snarled. 'You believe yourself to be something you are not. You are nothing but a powerless and nameless human boy, with no business living in a world such as this.'

The someone wailed.

The Snow Queen faded into nothing and the cathedral crumbled around her ghostly impression. With newfound certainty, the someone flew into the canopy, soaring higher than the trees, then higher than the spires that had stood a moment before. She passed the clouds and escaped the falling snow, to where the atmosphere touches the universe. There, she paused to shout to the unseen world, 'I am not who you think I am.'

In that moment, the someone found her name. 'I am Innocence,' she bellowed. She embodied the virtue.

The fierce wind ripped doorways between the worlds, through which tiny specks of ugly reflection and wicked thought were thrust by the tempest. Innocence could see herself reflected in the infinite colours of the kaleidoscope, the colours of worlds she did not recognise and faces that somehow resembled hers.

Innocence soared between the fragments of herself, seeking understanding, but each person she saw was transfixed by the joys and struggles of their own experiences. She longed to return home, but was unsure if she was welcome.

This was the moment I left the darkroom, bundles of her photographs still in my hands, and stepped out into the snow. 'Innocence,' I shouted into the storm. My love's new name felt unfamiliar on my tongue, yet perfectly appropriate. 'Please come home.'

My cry was drowned by Innocence's uncertainty as she questioned the name she had been certain of moments before. She had shattered her own reflection, and now its wickedness alighted the eyes and hearts of those from many worlds who dealt cruelty upon people that she recognised as fragments of herself. Lost in the tempest and certain of her guilt, Innocence tumbled through a crack in the clouds and fell with the snow into a new world.

I knew so much of Innocence's journey, yet I was unsure which world my love had escaped into, my heart tugging me across the sky towards each of her likenesses. Impulsively, I followed the pull into a forest like ours, but filled with the fragrances of spring, hoping to find a place where the perfume was interrupted by the scent of whiskey and film.

2

TEALE

Teale's feet appeared distorted, shattered like a
mirror beneath the surface of the transparent
river. Streams from the sea and from her glassy eyes
filled the waterway with salt. Her shaking fingers
stifled her tears. She sniffed.

Her trembling breaths slowly gave way to shallow
silence, but still she could hear heaving sobs. With
swollen eyes, she sought their owner.

To her left, burdocks rose high, swaying stems of
identical length moving as one in the breeze; to her
right, a flat expanse, desolate, the burning fingers
of a grass fire having scorched the life out of the
earth, reaching all the way to the bank.

Something made the brush shudder so that
it scratched her arm, brittle spikelets breaking
her skin like sharp words. A tiny, feathered body
appeared at the water's edge, hiccoughing sadness.

Teale watched the fluffy ball for a moment, but it
didn't seem to notice her.

'Hello there,' Teale said, her voice as soft as the
grey down that covered the little creature.

The bundle tremored, startled by the sound. It turned and noticed Teale, eyes widening.

'Please don't kick me,' the bird said.

'Why would I do that?' Teale replied.

'That's what the other girl used to do, in the poultry yard, while the ducks pecked and tormented me.' He lifted a grey wing to show his feathers, some crumpled and torn.

'Oh, you poor thing,' Teale said.

'Well, don't worry—I won't kick you. And those ducks won't hurt you anymore.'

The little bird looked at himself in the water. 'But it's not just those ducks that hate me,' he said. 'The wild ducks who live in the green and purple heather of the moors mocked me too. I am truly the ugliest duckling that ever did hatch.'

'Ugly? They call you ugly?'

The bird bowed his black and orange-striped beak towards the damp ground. 'Even my mother, though she defended me at first, eventually grew tired of the storm clouds that I carry in my down. Everyone calls me the Ugly Duckling.'

'Then there must be something in their eyes, distorting their sight,' Teale declared, 'or something in their hearts, making them cold and unkind. You are certainly not ugly and that simply won't do. We need to find you a real name.'

'Right now all I want is something to eat. I fled the poultry yard because of how they teased me, but at least there I could always beg for grain.'

'Then we will find you a name and some grain, too,' Teale said. 'Come on.' She pulled her legs from the water, dashing her reflection. Specks of dirt and blades of grass stuck to her bare feet as she climbed the bank. The world was large—too large for her—but she hoped this little bird might find somewhere to belong in the town that cast her out.

'Do we have to stray so far from the water?' the duckling asked as he clambered up the hill. 'I much prefer swimming.'

'I could carry you if you like,' Teale offered.

'No thank you,' the duckling said, struck by pride. 'It was just a question.'

'It might be as wet as the river here soon enough, in any case,' Teale said, looking over the distant cottages to where clouds the colour of the duckling's down were rolling like the ocean waves Teale had seen in the pages of picture books.

The rain fell before the two of them reached the town. The bird opened his beak to the heavens to catch the droplets. After a moment, he said, 'They always called me a duckling, but perhaps I'm not. Perhaps I am a cloud, fallen from the sky.'

'Then I will call you Cloud,' said Teale, 'if that pleases you.'

Cloud nodded, chuffed to have a name of his very own.

The approaching storm bothered Cloud little, but Teale shivered as her clothes clung to her skin. The first of a smattering of cottages denoted the outskirts of the town and offered walls of smooth logs and a roof of woven grass, and hopefully warm shelter. The duckling hopped up the timber stairs as Teale tapped her knuckles against the heavy door.

A crack of flickering light appeared at the edge of the panel, and a face seemingly streaked by the same wooden grain peered out into the damp. 'Yes?' the woman asked.

'I'm sorry to bother you,' Teale said, 'but we are seeking protection from the rain. We were wondering if we could rest here for a moment; hopefully it will pass shortly.'

'We?' the woman asked, looking over Teale's shoulder.

Teale gestured to her feet where Cloud was hiding, shivering.

'Is it cursed by the melancholy of the storm?' asked the woman. 'Or does it always look this ugly?' Nevertheless, she invited them inside.

Cloud shuffled across the timber with clumsy feet and was met by the black and gold plumage that he recognised from the poultry yard. A queenly comb slumped over preened feathers, and stern eyes scrutinised him from blood-red caruncles. 'What are you?' the hen asked.

Proud of his new name, the bird happily replied, 'I'm Cloud.'

A nimble body leapt from the dining table and landed before the two birds. The cat's tail swept the floor. 'But what are you,' he growled.

Ashamed to be an ugly duckling but knowing nothing else, he shrugged his dishevelled wings. 'Nothing,' he replied. 'Just Cloud.'

'You must be something,' the cat said.

'Besides soaking wet,' the hen clucked.

The duckling's body quaked, ripples flowing down his downy back as he tossed droplets of water across the kitchen.

'Now, don't do that,' the hen said.

'The woman won't allow it,' the cat added.

'And rightly so!' the hen squawked. 'She doesn't scrub these floors just to have some ugly little bird wander in and speckle the timber with its filth.'

'Sorry,' Cloud said.

'What will you do to redeem yourself?' the cat asked.

'Can you lay eggs?' asked the hen.

'No,' said Cloud.

The hen clucked and drew lines on the floor panels, scratching as though they were earth.

'Can you raise your back, or purr, or throw out sparks?' asked the cat.

Cloud shook his head.

'Then what do you have to offer?' the hen asked.

'Nothing,' the cat replied before Cloud had a chance to open his beak.

'This should help,' the woman said, placing a bag of seed between Teale and herself.

'Thank you,' Teale said. 'He was getting awfully hungry.'

'They look to be getting on,' the woman suggested, sitting down to a mug of hot chocolate.

Cloud's feathers, skewed by the storm and still damaged from past encounters, were a ceaseless reminder of the little bird's hardships. Teale heard the judgemental whispers of the other animals, but the woman seemed oblivious. 'I hope so,' Teale said.

'I'm sure my loves are being nothing but generous,' the woman replied, 'even though he's covering my floor with mud.'

'Sorry,' Teale said. 'It is truly a miserable day.'

'I don't think it's the day that makes your bird look so miserable.'

'I feel sorry for him. I know how it hurts to feel like you don't belong,' Teale said, looking down at the impression of her face, spiralling atop her own steaming chocolate, the sweet but bitter liquid consuming her features.

'Don't be silly,' said the woman. 'You look just like any other young girl—you're not nearly as ugly.'

'Are you a hen?' the cat asked, stalking Cloud beneath the dining table.

Cloud stumbled over his slate feet, his webbed toes leaving behind slippery triangles.

'Don't even joke about that,' the hen screeched. 'No relative of mine could ever be responsible for something so...'

'I know. I was only joking,' said the cat, licking his lips, his rump swaying.

Cloud closed his eyes, preparing for the rush of the cat's pounce, the momentary agony as jaws locked around his fragile neck.

Warmth enveloped him and lifted him from the ground.

'Leave him alone,' Teale said, cradling Cloud in her hands. 'How dare you torment somebody just because he's not sure where he belongs.'

'I'm sure they meant no harm,' the woman said.

The cat's grin stretched wide, his eyes glinting with fragments of fractured glass. The hen pecked at the floor.

'We best be off,' Teale said. She took the bag of seed and abandoned her lukewarm reflection, returning to the rain with Cloud against her chest. The wind blew the deluge sideways, the assault of droplets striking her skin like shards of glass. She bowed her head against the attack, seeking cover.

'I'm sorry for leaving you alone with those wicked

creatures,' Teale said as she darted across the grass, muddied water splattering her legs.

An incoherent sound escaped Cloud's throat as he burrowed his beak into Teale's shirt. She covered his body with her warm hand, coaxing him to stop shaking.

He didn't look up until the rain softened, blocked by the canopy.

'I thought you were taking us into the town,' Cloud said.

'The town abandoned me a long time ago,' Teale said, 'and it seems those close-minded people will offer you little respite. We're better off travelling through the forest. Perhaps there will be another village, full of kinder folk.'

'So long as we don't go near the poultry yard,' Cloud said, before burying his beak in the bag of grain.

Once he'd eaten enough, Teale lowered him onto fallen leaves and he waddled towards the nearest puddle, splashing in water too dirty to cast a reflection.

'It's not quite the river,' Teale said.

Cloud didn't seem to mind as he whirled around a puddle just deep enough for his webbed feet. 'I never thought I'd swim again,' he called.

Teale traversed a winding path through the forest while Cloud fluttered and splashed between the puddles left in the trenches among the ferns. When they reached a point where the path branched out in many directions like a great tree, Cloud looked at Teale expectantly, but she didn't know where they were going. 'I've never journeyed this far from the town before,' she said.

'So we're lost?' Cloud asked.

'Not lost,' replied Teale, 'just thinking. We are heroes who have arrived at a crossroads; we need only make a decision.'

Cloud sniffed at the mud leading ahead, then to the left and the right. 'This way,' he decided.

Teale wanted only to put distance between herself and the town, so was happy to follow the little bird's lead. All the same, she was curious. 'What's this way?' she asked.

'I'm not sure,' Cloud said. 'The path just smelt... unfamiliar. I like unfamiliar.'

'So do I,' Teale smiled.

'We have lots in common,' Cloud observed, a skip in his waddle.

'We do,' Teale replied.

'When you were in that woman's house, I heard you say that you know how it feels not to belong. I don't understand though—you look just like every other girl I know. Or, at least, the one at the poultry yard.'

'Sometimes it's not about how we look.'

'You mean like how the girl in the poultry yard used to hurt me, but you don't?'

Teale smiled. 'I guess that's one difference.'

Cloud splashed ahead, distracted by the water. Eventually he asked, 'What else is there?'

Teale took a breath, assembling and reassembling sentences on her tongue. 'Well,' she began, 'Once upon a time, I fell in love. That wasn't altogether unusual and nobody was surprised; most people just wanted to know the name of "the lucky man". Some tried to guess. "Perhaps it's Cordell, the merchant's son," they said. "He's handsome." And yes, he is handsome—in fact, I had a fling with him once when we were younger—but we can't help who we fall in love with. Her name was Violet.'

Cloud returned to the path while Teale spoke, taking four waddling steps for each of her strides. 'What's love?' he asked.

A scratchy, squawking noise interrupted Teale's reply. Cloud's little legs began to shake, no longer able to carry him forwards. 'What was that?' he whispered.

'Sounded like some sort of bird. Did we accidentally find the path to the poultry yard?'

'I don't think any of the birds there sound like that,' Cloud said. He lowered his shivering beak closer to the mud. 'Anyway, it doesn't smell right here,' he added.

'Maybe it's the moor, and those wild ducks you mentioned.'

Another squawk punctuated the air, followed by some clicking and splashing. 'No, that doesn't sound right,' Cloud said. 'I've never heard noises like those before.'

'Well, let's go and investigate,' Teale said. She rushed ahead before Cloud could disagree, turning a corner and revealing a scene that had been hidden behind a curtain of trees.

The river ballooned, creating a sparkling pool that flowed around several large, white bodies. They opened and closed their wings, snapped at each other's long necks, and squawked at the sky. The storm had cleared, streaks of blue peering through the opening overhead.

'They're so graceful,' Cloud said from behind Teale's ankle.

'They are,' Teale agreed. 'Maybe you should go and speak to them. They might be able to help you.'

'You think?'

'Worth a try,' Teale said.

Trembling, trusting, Cloud waddled into the open and down towards the water. He tumbled from the bank into himself. A collection of long, thin necks twisted so their owners could scrutinise his tiny, grey body.

Stillness descended on the pool, with nothing disturbing the surface but the gentle current and the silent trail left by Cloud's gliding form. Feeling unworthy to look at the faces ahead, he kept his head bowed, staring at his own sad eyes, when a flurry of movement sent ripples through the water. 'They've grown tired of staring at the ugly bird that dared to swim across their pool,' Cloud said to his reflection, 'and they've decided to kill us.'

Teale watched as the elegant birds parted so that a number of downy grey balls could splash and chatter through the water. They swam over to Cloud and gathered around him, heads tilted this way and that. When Cloud looked up, expecting to see orange bills and angry eyes, he was confused to see faces not unlike his own.

'Play with us!' one bird said.

'Yes, please play with us,' another agreed.

'Then we'll have even numbers!' said a third.

The others nodded and laughed as they swam dizzying circles around Cloud.

'Hold on, children,' one of the larger birds said, gliding gracefully over to where they were gathered. She bent to examine Cloud. 'But where are you from? I've never seen you before.'

'I'm not from anywhere, anymore,' Cloud said.

'You must be from somewhere. How did you get here?' the bird prodded.

Cloud, scared of upsetting the creature, opened his beak and more words tumbled out. 'I used to live in the poultry yard, but I didn't belong with the other ducklings. I fled into the forest and found the wild ducks in the moor, but they told me I was ugly and that I didn't belong with them either. Then I met Teale by the river.' He glanced back at Teale, who was now sitting on the bank, toes breaking the smooth surface of the water. She nodded encouragingly.

'Of course you didn't fit in with the ducklings,' said the bird. 'You're a cygnet.'

'A... cygnet?'

'A baby swan. One of us,' said one of the other cygnets.

'So can he play with us?' a second cygnet asked the swan.

'Please, can he stay?' a third begged.

'Sure,' one of the swans said. 'He can stay for as long as he likes.'

Cloud was bombarded with the pleading of his friends. 'Come and play!' one said.

'Stay forever!' another suggested.

Cloud peered at the faces that looked just like his own. 'Okay,' he said.

There was cheering and delight from the cygnets, and even the swans seemed pleased. Cloud had never been so happy or felt so welcome.

Well, except during his time with Teale.

'But there's something I need to do first,' Cloud said.

The cygnets heaved sighs but the swans seemed to understand, shaking their heads at the children and telling them to hush. Cloud turned his back on his new family and crossed the pool. Teale was still sitting on the bank in the fading light, smiling.

'Did it go well?' she asked when Cloud was close enough to hear.

'They look just like me,' Cloud said, the shock yet to wear off.

'They have about as much energy as you as well,' Teale laughed.

'Why did you wait here, all this time?' Cloud asked.

'It's nice to see you happy,' she replied. 'Better than sitting by the river alone, like I was when I first met you.'

'They told me I can stay with them,' Cloud said. 'And I think I will. I never dreamed of this much happiness when I was still in the poultry yard or alone in the forest.'

'I'm glad you've found your home.'

'You'll find one too,' Cloud said. 'I'm sure of it.'

'Thank you,' Teale said. 'Now, off you go. They're waiting for you!'

The cluster of white and grey glowed like a beacon at the centre of the pool, guiding Cloud towards his new life, but something made him turn back. 'You know what you said before?' he said. 'About the girl you loved?'

'Yes.'

'Before, when they asked me to stay, the cygnets said they love me. If this is what love feels like, then I think you should be able to love anyone you like.'

Teale's eyes shone glassy like the surface of the pool in the light of the rising moon.

3
AMBER

Once I reached the edge of the kingdom, I turned towards the stone and brick that I once called my home. Only the spire stood taller than the orchard, reflecting the sharp light of the sunrise.

Every morning I had watched a familiar, silent scene through the window of the spire, and it was not difficult to imagine the vision as I continued along the course of the river. My stepmother stood in her chambers, and I imagined her speaking to her ghastly looking-glass. I wondered what she might be saying, and if her mirror ever replied.

I've never had much time for mirrors. I've always preferred to admire my mud-streaked cheeks in the uncertain reflections of the river. Every time I washed my callused hands in its rushing water, I wondered how far that river ran. The river was a snake, and every step along its writhing form took me further from the venom of my stepmother.

The river led me through trees unlike any I had ever seen. They grew sparsely at first, but then tightened like the rows of the orchard, before moving closer still like the forests I had read about in stories. The sun was blotted out of the sky until I could only see the closest trunks, and the narrow path between them, which gradually steered me away from the river. I felt as though days and nights could pass unseen in this darkness, and perhaps they did.

Through the shadows, I eventually saw a cottage, and tentatively I approached. Garden beds filled with struggling plants were built against worn mudbrick walls. I was several paces from the door when I noticed that it was being nudged open by a curious fox.

I followed the creature to the open doorway and peered inside the cottage, considering the leaf-strewn floor. The timber boards were warped and, in some places, eaten by the moisture of the forest. The place seemed abandoned.

Guided by the fox, I entered the abandoned cottage, but the creature was unseen and I suspected it disappeared into the shadows or left through one of the window-like holes in the mudbrick walls. I brushed away debris from a square of relatively dry, undamaged wood.

There, I stretched out, and looked at the dimly lit trees through the window until I was looking at the darkness behind my eyelids.

I awoke to voices.

'Who is she?'

'What is she doing here?' 'Pebbles seems to like her.'

'I don't care if Pebbles likes her—she's trespassing!'

'Hold on—she's waking up.'

Seven faces crowded around me as I struggled

to sit up, disturbing the fox who must have fallen asleep while curled against my torso.

'Are you okay?' somebody asked.

I could not recall the last time I was asked such a question.

🍎

Flame lit the kindling in the fire pit and we sat around it. Cave tended to a pot of soup while Hawk questioned our intruder. 'We aren't going to hurt you,' he said. 'Speak for yourself,' Stone interjected.

'Don't worry about him,' Hawk said. 'He gets grumpy when he's hungry. But don't be scared. What is your name?'

'I do not have a name anymore, but before she died my mother called me Amber.' 'I can tell from your dress that you are not from the forest. Are you lost, Amber?'

'Sort of.'

'How can somebody be "sort of" lost?' Stone asked. 'I'm sort of lost,' Sky said absently.

'I do not know my way home, but that does not matter, for I do not wish to return,' Amber said.

'And where is home?' Hawk asked. 'The palace.'

'Were you a farmhand? A kitchen maid?'

'I often worked on the farms and in the kitchens, but I was not servant. I was the princess,' Amber said.

'If this girl is a runaway princess, we should ransom her back to the palace,' Stone suggested.

'We are not ransoming a poor, scared woman to the palace when she clearly needs help,' Hawk said.

'Then how do you suppose we feed ourselves?

We're nearly out of money for the markets and Thunderstorm's gardens are as empty as our pockets.'

'Amber said she worked in the farm at the palace. Perhaps she can stay and help us?' Branches suggested.

'If she would like to,' Hawk added.

The fire painted streaks across the garden—my garden—and, as Amber nodded, my space was relinquished and my feelings disregarded. I disappeared into the shadows and crept inside the cottage.

🍎

I accompanied the forest-dwellers to the market where they sold the wooden carvings, fine fabrics, and precious gemstones they had crafted or collected. As we walked, I attempted to remember the names of my companions.

Sky led the way, named after the way her mind floated among the clouds. Hawk followed, nudging her gently onto the correct trail as she became distracted by the flowers or misled by her memory. Flame was the loudest, shouting and joking with the others, but when he became too jovial it was Stone who yelled at him to be quiet. Cave and Branches spoke in hushed tones about the stones and sewing they carried. Then there was Thunderstorm; they trailed behind and said nothing at all.

'I'm sorry they asked me to help in your garden,' I said.

Thunderstorm did not reply.

'I do not wish to take away a place that I can see is important to you, but I also cannot be sent back to the palace. Last night after you left the fireside, the others promised me a bed if I could help the garden grow, to keep your stomachs full and pockets heavy. I have never encountered such generosity before.'

'I understand that you need a place to stay so that you are protected from the palace,' Thunderstorm whispered, 'but what about what I need?'

'What do you need, Thunderstorm?'

'I need my garden. I will not let you steal it.'

'I do not wish to steal your garden, Thunderstorm. I only hope to help it thrive, and to help you tend to it.'

🍎

I considered Amber's words while I lay in my bed, unable to sleep. I did not wish to share my gardens with a stranger, but I did long to see my vegetables flourish. I spent the night attempting to reconcile these two feelings—resentment that Amber had been invited into my space, and joy that she could potentially save it.

The first beams of sunrise were accompanied by the sound of shuffling in the hall. Amber passed my doorway, her hair knotted atop her head. I heard the door open as she walked out into the morning. The thought of her sitting alone among the plants made my stomach twist, so I followed her.

We sat in the soil, my mouth filled with bitterness and hope. Amber inspected each plant, leaning so close to the stems and leaves that they brushed against her nose.

'These potatoes and broccoli plants need more sunlight,' she said as she clawed at the soil. 'And those lettuce heads would be better suited to the shade. The trees here are blocking the rain, and that's leaving the clay too dry.'

That first morning, I believed Amber's words were for herself, but as I rose with her each sunrise and watched her move plants from one garden bed to another, or fetch buckets of water from the river, I realised that her commentary was for me. She did not want the garden to herself; she was teaching me to reclaim it.

🍎

As the first of the plants began to heal, their dying leaves opened and they turned to face the sun. Each fragment of green helped to erode the wall between me and Thunderstorm, and each day they seemed to sit closer as I worked.

'Would you like to help?' I asked. 'What can I do?'

With gentle hands, I taught Thunderstorm to relocate the last of the struggling stems. That evening, when lightning streaked the sky and thunder made the roof rattle, I glimpsed Thunderstorm lying back against the pillows of their bed, a smile on their face as their namesake helped the plants settle into new homes.

On drier days, we carried water from the river together, and I showed Thunderstorm how much each plant needed to spread its roots through the soil. We also carried river- smoothed stones, denoting the edges of the garden bed with greys and blues and browns.

'If you were one of these river stones, which one would you be?' Thunderstorm asked.

The question was unlike anything I had heard before, and was spoken with such sincerity that I hardly knew how to answer.

'I think I would be this stone,' Thunderstorm said in my silence, a flat, grey pebble in their outstretched hand. They flipped it over, revealing the way its colour faded to black.

The passing months brought warmth between us and to the soil. The spring encouraged weeds to crowd the empty spaces in the garden, and at dawn we would sit with our knees touching, tugging the interlopers from the soil.

As the plants thrived, the scent of delicious produce spread beneath the undergrowth and brought visitors from afar. Rabbits snuck into the garden, disregarding the river stones and stealing more than their share of crops.

Thunderstorm held my hand and led me through the forest, where we sought fallen branches and bundles of tall grass. We built fences tied with dry stems and spent the evenings wrapping cloth around our sore, blistered fingers. Soon the garden yielded more than we could eat, and we carried baskets of leftover produce with us to the market to sell alongside the wooden carvings, fine fabrics, and precious gemstones.

Thunderstorm would never accept the kind words spoken about their produce. They would respond to compliments by saying, 'Amber knows how to nudge the leaves of timid saplings towards the sky, and how to sing melodies until their delicate bodies are laden with produce. She knows how crops follow the seasons like the birds flee the cold. She knows how to read the clouds and when to disrupt the earth to ensure a bountiful harvest.'

But I would respond. 'The plants only thrive because of the passion and love with which Thunderstorm tends to their garden.'

'Our garden,' they would correct.

One morning, as the sun rose before Amber did, I knew she must be unwell. Her skin felt warmer to my touch than the summer that pressed against our bedroom window. Amber insisted on walking with me to the market—as was our routine—but I refused her company.

'Sleep,' I said. 'Look after yourself so you can feel better when I return.'

I offered Amber a bowl of water, kissed her on her blushing cheek, and left the house with the others.

I had never been alone inside the cottage, and the silence that descended made me more uncomfortable than my fever. I slept to avoid it, and once I woke, the sun had traced its path across the sky and was directly overhead. A crisp knock on the door reverberated through the hollow halls.

The cottage had been my home through the last days of frost, the blooms of spring, and the humid days of early summer, yet I'd never seen a passer-by stray this far from the forest path. When I shuffled to the door and nudged it open, I was surprised to see an unfamiliar face.

'Hello, darling,' said the woman, a basket in her hands not unlike the one with which I carried produce to the markets. 'Would you like to buy my apples?'

The red globes sparkled in her basket, but I had no money to call my own. 'I'm sorry, but I cannot,' I replied. 'Why not go to the markets and sell them to the travellers and creatures of the forest?'

'I prefer the personal touch,' the woman replied. 'Please try an apple, free of charge. You look awfully pale—perhaps the sugar will help you.'

I tried to refuse the woman's generous offer, but she pressed an apple into my hand and would not leave until I brought it to my lips. My apple's flesh tasted bitter, like rust. It stuck in my throat and a gasp escaped me. In the moment before I collapsed, I recognised the woman's eyes.

I stood before the looking-glass gifted to me by my father. There I saw a palimpsest, my reflection layered atop the visage of my late husband, and of all the men before him. I stared into the mirror, and the mirror stared back, fragments of reflection glittering in my eyes.

'Amber is far superior to you, Queen Leda,' the mirror said. 'You have always known it.

Everybody in the kingdom loves her.'

'Only because she goes into the fields and covers

herself with mud and grime so they believe that she is one of them.'

'And yet, even covered in mud and grime, she is far prettier than you,' the mirror said. 'But is she as clever? I think not. I am the one who stole the kingdom from her, marrying her father and taking my place as queen.'

'And yet she manages to foil every attempt you make on her life, even when she sleeps.' 'But my threats and attempts have scared her from the kingdom.'

'Amber has come of age. She is now old enough to challenge you for the throne,' the mirror said. 'She may have left, but can you be sure that she has left forever? Perhaps she is gathering the support of the people before she rises against you.'

'Then I must be rid of her,' I replied. 'Though I do not know where to look.'

'She fled into the forest and is residing in a cottage. This is where you might find her.' 'Still, I do not know what I will do when I get there.'

My reflection smiled, reached outside of the frame, and returned with an apple grasped between their fingers. Its skin glowed blood red.

I coughed. Something stuck in my throat.

The sun of a new summer day kissed my skin through a new silk dress. I could smell the flowers that Thunderstorm and I had planted between the vegetables in our garden. I felt the grain of a coffin beneath my hands, and heard Thunderstorm weep. I longed to comfort them, but my consciousness was trapped behind my eyes.

Worried conversations and melancholic monologues sounded distant in the dark behind my eyelids, as though I were floating beneath the surface of a river. A horse's hooves approached, like a pebble skimming across the surface.

And then I heard you. 'That maiden is the most beautiful creature I have ever laid eyes on,' you said.

'She was more beautiful when she was alive,' Thunderstorm responded.

'I want to take her to my castle and encase her in glass so that her red lips can bring me happiness each time I look at them,' you said.

'Our friend has died and you want to take her dead body away so you can stare at her?' Stone asked.

'Not just me,' you continued, 'but my entire kingdom. Do not be selfish—she could bring joy to hundreds of people. What do you want for her? I could give you jewels, riches...' 'We don't want anything,' Hawk said.

'Excellent.'

'No!' Thunderstorm exclaimed. 'He didn't mean that you can take her; she is not for sale.'

Hands wrapped around the edges of the open coffin, fingertips brushing against my skin. A war was fought over my motionless body. I was tossed overboard, landing on the leaf litter, the wind knocked from my lungs.

I coughed and spat, a piece of bitter flesh landing beside your shiny shoes.

🍎

I looked upon Amber, my love—curled upon the leaves, crippled but breathing—and was filled with wordless joy.

🍎

'I still don't understand why you're telling me all of this,' the prince says.

'Is it not clear?' I reply. 'You want me to come with you so that you and your subjects can stare at my lifeless face, but why would I leave the life I've built here for somebody I've only just met?'

'I could offer you a title. Don't you want to be a princess again?'

'I have grown tired of how royalty seem to handle their disagreements.'

'Can you not picture your beautiful face parading through the kingdom beside my handsome visage? Do you not find me attractive?'

'If beauty were only the shape of a face and my circumstances were different, perhaps your image would tempt me back to a castle, but your intentions are selfish and your personality is unappealing, and it masks the gentle colour of your eyes.'

'You expect me to believe that you would rather stay here with these... dwarfs?' the prince asks.

'Come on, it's time for us to go.'

'No, it's time for you to go.'

The humidity draws beads of sweat across my brow, but Thunderstorm still holds me against their skin. 'I thought I'd lost you,' they whisper.

'And I you,' I reply. 'It broke my heart to hear your sadness.'

'I never want to feel that ache again.'

'I love you, Thunderstorm.'
'I love you too.'

4
VIOLET

Words dissolved into a string of melodious syllables, incomprehensible but for their beauty. The ballad overwhelmed the birdsong, permeating the deepest corners of the dense forest, tickling tree tops and echoing beneath bridges. A prince heard the hypnotic tune and was drawn towards it, entranced.

He happened upon a tower, like that which might rise from a castle. It had no door, and a singular window, out of reach. He tied his pale horse to a tree and hid behind the bushes, looking up into the shadowy opening as dusk struck the surrounding canopy.

The melody continued, coaxing the moon out of hiding and encouraging its gentle glow. Silver light dusted the tips of the swaying grasses that circled the tower's base. Among these long blades, a troll with skin of milky green was camouflaged, invisible if not for her call.

'Who is it that sings so magically that their notes resonate beneath the bridges and stir my soul?' the troll called up to the tower, infinitely braver than the prince who falsely blamed his hesitation on his desire to not interrupt.

The song ended, as they inevitably do, and a face—exquisite in its plainness—was illuminated in the tower's open window. 'Who is it that calls to me from the night?' the girl responded.

'I lost my name many years ago, beneath a bridge in another world. I hadn't any need for it anymore, so I tossed it in the river.'

'But without a name, how do you know who you are?'

'I am more than a name, my dear,' the troll said. 'As are you. In this forest that has always offered me so little, your gentle voice was a beacon through the eve. I knew I must find you, the girl who holds such melancholy in her heart and sings such sadness with her tongue. If names are so important, tell me: what is the name of the girl who shatters the darkness with her sad song?'

'My name is Violet.'

The following night, Violet's voice floated through the forest like the scent of a freshly-baked dessert resting on a window sill. The troll stumbled across the undergrowth, following the sound. She called to the girl from the same place she had stood the previous night, and the prince watched from the undergrowth.

'Tell me, my dear,' called the troll. 'What is it that weighs down your heart?'

'I am hideous,' cried Violet. 'It is for this reason that I must remain here, locked in my tower. To force myself upon the world would be to do them such harm.'

'I am forbidden to roam the forest in the daylight, to avoid exposing the world to the totality of my features. Does the dull orb of the moon shine brightly enough to reveal my face? Hideous is a foolish name that I have been called by those who have chased me with flames and forks, but those tyrants daren't speak ill of a girl with long, golden hair such as yourself.'

'It is not my hair that concerns me,' Violet replied. 'I do not need to have skin as green as yours to be deemed too ugly to be seen by humankind.'

'Who was the wicked fool who told you such a thing? I know hideous, and I know it is a quality that you do not embody.'

'You do not know me at all.'

The troll returned with the moon the following night, and the prince returned too, watching with shy eyes. 'If I do not know you,' the troll said, interrupting Violet's song, 'then teach me.'

'I was left here by my father when I turned eighteen,' Violet said. 'With weathered hands, he built this tower around me, with only a window through which to see the world. I asked him if he was saving me from the dangers that occupy the corners of the forest, but he shook his head; a piece of fractured glass sparkled in his angry eyes as he told me that he was keeping the rest of the world safe from me. He told me that I was an anomaly, that I was not normal and could never be.'

'And what could your crime have possibly been?'

'My father discovered my love for a girl in the village.'

'That was your wrongdoing? You fell in love?'

'But it was much worse than simply that,' Violet exclaimed. 'I had fallen for boys when I was younger, and yet suddenly I was a girl in love with another girl. So, my father left me here to die.'

'And yet you survived. Tell me, how?'

'The song that called to you through the forest calls to others. The birds bring me gifts of water and food. They ensure my survival, though I sometimes wonder if they needn't bother.'

'The birds cannot be controlled. They only help those whom they deem worthy. If you were not worthy, they would not come.'

Clouds hid the moon the following night. Violet's song pierced the sky until midnight, and the prince listened, eyes glistening. He had longed to return to the tower in the daylight, when the troll would be hidden beneath her bridge, but found himself inventing royal responsibilities to keep himself trapped at the palace until dusk.

Even now, with the troll nowhere to be seen, he could not convince himself to speak to Violet. He chastised himself for his cowardice until the troll appeared in the tall grass.

'I have returned, just as the birds return to their roost each night. I wanted to tell you that there are many reasons that I could be considered hideous, but who I love is not one of them. Before I came to live in this forest, I loved many: some trolls, some humans, some men, some women, and some inhabiting the liminal spaces. Sometimes the world does not understand that love is to be celebrated, no matter who it is felt between. Some people believe the affairs of others somehow concern them,' she said.

'You and I are alike?'

'In some ways,' the troll replied. 'Let me tell you a story of a girl who loved many, but also loved few. Who was confronted by the ignorance of the world and defended herself against it. Perhaps it will help you see that you are not alone, and that you are certainly not hideous.'

Many years ago, on the outskirts of a forest not unlike the one we now inhabit, first light painted the canopy.

5
SIENNA

There had been a typhoon. The rain had lasted twenty-one days, trapping the village folk in their homes with nothing to eat but stale bread and old vegetables. Those who had tried to visit the closed stores in the village square had returned home with empty baskets and battered faces.

That morning, the baker had a queue to serve and not enough pastries. Though his shelves were bare, he had kept her usual order aside, and passed her the hamper of biscuits and wine as soon as he noticed her crimson coat. I am unsure what he said to her. 'Give my best to Bella,' perhaps. Sienna nodded.

A forest bordered the village, and the memory of rain continued to fall from the leaf-cup cradles as they rocked in the incensed breeze. Dust motes danced in the sunrise, and clouds of silver mist floated between the treetops. Sienna walked with her nose to the sky, admiring the first rays of golden light to warm her skin in weeks.

The forest was not my home by choice, but it was my home, with trees dense enough to hide my hideous features from the sunlight—but Sienna knew it just as well as I did. Every day when the sky was clear, she would trace the winding path to Bella's house with delicious treats to share.

The carpet of leaves, usually ablaze with crackling reds and oranges, was muddied and soft. The trees were crying sap from where the storms had split them open. Sienna stepped into shrubs overflowing with tiny flowers to avoid the water-filled trenches that scarred the barren path.

'It's dangerous to stray from the trail, little lady.' A wolf with gravel in his throat and shining grey eyes sat on a boulder, so dirty that Sienna didn't notice him until he spoke.

'I know my way,' she replied.

'I'm sure you do,' the wolf said. He leapt from the rock as Sienna passed and fell into stride with her. 'But where is your way taking you?'

Sienna knew that speaking to such a wolf was dangerous, but that angering him by refusing to answer his question may put her at further risk.

'My girlfriend's house,' she replied. She hoped her words would send him back into the muddy hole that he dragged himself from. He smelt of decomposing leaves.

'You know what you could do instead of visiting your friend?' he growled.

Sienna dodged the wolf's yellow gaze as she had learnt to do in the marketplace, avoiding the hawking and heckling of merchants.

The wolf didn't allow Sienna to evade him for long, bounding ahead and blocking her path with his width. 'You could spend the day with me,' he said.

'No, thank you,' Sienna responded firmly, stepping past him.

'You'd rather spend the day with some girl than with me?' he asked, walking with her.

'I'd rather spend the day with anyone over you,' Sienna muttered.

They walked silently for several paces, Sienna's hands turning pale as they clutched the handle of her basket. I contemplated intervening, but the light was brighter across the path and I knew I would only scare Sienna with my countenance.

'This girl must be some friend,' the wolf said.

'Yes, she's my *girlfriend*,' Sienna reiterated.

'Oh!' the wolf exclaimed. 'You know, I've cured lesbians before. It's well known that all lesbians are just waiting for the right guy to come along. How do you know you don't like men if you've never been with one?'

'Who says I haven't? Or that I'm a lesbian?'

The tree trunks began to press closer, blocking the wolf's attempts to walk beside Sienna. She felt his stale breath on the back of her neck.

'You said you were a lesbian,' he said. 'You just told me—you have a girlfriend!'

Sienna sighed. She turned and faced the wolf, immediately regretting it as he leaned towards her. She retreated. 'I am attracted to men *and* women,' she said. 'And all other genders, while we're on the topic.'

'Bisexual, eh?' the wolf said with a wink.

'Pansexual, actually,' Sienna corrected as she resumed walking.

'I knew you wanted me!' the wolf said, triumphant.

Sienna was so astounded that she laughed. The sound was harsh, humourless.

'How do you figure that?'

'You just admitted that you're attracted to everyone. And you bisexuals or pansexuals or whatever can have sex with as many people as you like, right?'

'Are you serious? Just because I can be attracted to all genders doesn't mean I want to sleep with everyone I see, and all at once. That sort of life might make some people happy, but my perfectly fine, *monogamous* relationship is enough work for me, thank you very much.'

'No need to be rude,' the wolf said, his long canines glistening. 'You should smile more.'

The wolf hurried ahead through the undergrowth, putting bitter distance between himself and Sienna; she dawdled, observing the cushions of toadstools that had appeared after the rain.

I had never seen the wolf in my forest before, and I hoped never to see him again.

I wished to ensure Sienna was safe, and her crimson coat made tracing her line through the forest a simple task. I watched her pause by the lake, its banks eroded by the storms, and throw biscuit crumbs among the burdocks where the wild ducks gathered. Sienna examined herself in the still water and smiled.

I remember looking upon Sienna with envious eyes, jealous that she knew words that could hold the weight of her feelings and attractions, of her identity. At the time, my truth felt too heavy for such a word to exist, and I longed for the certainty that Sienna exuded.

Bella lived in a hut of wood and stone, her gardens filled with flowers and herbs in neat clusters that contrasted with the natural pattern of trees and ferns that circled the clearing.

Sienna tapped the grain of the wooden door with her knuckles and Bella recognised the sound. The door disappeared inward and a girl with her hair like a bird's nest—complete with feathers and twigs—appeared in the opening. She brought Sienna into her arms; the type of embrace that makes onlookers long to be held by those they love.

With Sienna safe, I sought to leave, but was brought to pause when I heard their conversation through the open shutters of the only window.

'Did you see a wolf while you were walking?' Bella asked. 'Sounded like he'd swallowed stones, his face matted with mud?'

'He followed me part of the way,' Sienna replied. 'How did you know?'

'He came to my door,' Bella said. 'Knocked and said he was you.'

Sienna coughed, attempting to fill her throat with shattered glass, and stretched herself taller. 'Hello, little lady. What a big chest you have!'

'Sounds like him,' Bella said, laughing at the parody. 'So, of course I told him that he wasn't fooling anyone.'

'I'm sure he responded well to that.'

'You know, the usual,' Bella replied. She crossed

to the counter and placed a handful of tea leaves into a pot. 'Told me I was missing out and that he could show me a good time.'

Sienna's laughter bubbled with the water boiling in the kettle.

'So I asked him, if women are so bad, why was he so desperate to sleep with one?' She slid a cup across the table, and the ceramic warmed Sienna's hands as Bella's words warmed her heart.

'Did he leave you alone after that?'

'Of course not,' Bella said. 'He started banging on the door so hard that I thought he might break it down.'

'So how did you get rid of him?'

'I asked if he wanted a cup of tea.'

'Belladonna!' she exclaimed, her full name slipping through Sienna's astounded lips.

'And he thought that sounded like a wonderful idea. At least, until I opened the door and tossed the tea across his torso.'

Though I had never before seen the wolf in my forest—and never did see him again—it was clear that Sienna and Bella had encountered many predators of his kind. And yet, it seemed that with their love of each other and certainty within themselves, it became easier to defend against such ignorance. Still, just as it had hurt me to be chased out of the forest by pitchfork-wielding villagers, I was sure their need to defend themselves was painful.

I wanted to be stronger. I sought to be strong enough to fight the injustice, rather than simply watch these two young women protect themselves against it. I sought to be strong enough to stand up to those who brandished their pitchforks and ignorance at those who were doing no harm, and perhaps right the wrongs of the world.

Sienna and Bella sipped tea and shared biscuits, and as clouds covered the sun and the rain began to fall again, they drank wine from their teacups and it warmed their souls. And I prepared to leave my forest forever.

❧

Silence fell upon the forest, with even the crickets pausing their rhythmic calls as Violet contemplated the story. Eventually, once the thoughts had fallen into place like confetti in a snow globe, Violet spoke.

'My father once told me that there was no one like me, and yet I see myself in Sienna and I see myself in you.'

'You are certainly not alone, my dear,' the troll replied.

'Did you ever find the word you sought, that could carry the weight of your truth?'

'I did. I rarely speak it aloud to others, but it helps me understand myself. I am *queer*.'

'Queer?' Violet tasted the label, letting it fill the hollows of her mouth and throat. 'I like how that sounds.'

'You are welcome to adopt it if it helps you make sense of the attractions you felt before your father brought you here, and those that you continue to feel.'

As pale light breached the canopy, the troll

realised that she had stayed too long telling stories of the place she once called home. She fled into the dawn, seeking shelter beneath the bridge before the sun truly rose.

With the moonlight the following evening came haunting notes of a softer song, like rain so light it may not be falling. When the troll arrived at the base of Violet's tower, she saw the sparkle of teeth among the stars, a glimpse of a smile.

'Your soul seems lighter, my dear,' the troll called, 'and your song has lost its crushing melancholy.'

'I have spent so many years here with only the birds and my uncertainty for company. You have brought me peace, and a word to tie my worries to. My father's parting thoughts still echo in my mind, but I have misplaced their significance.'

'I am pleased to have helped you,' the troll replied.

'Will you stop spending your evenings here with me now that you have held your mirror to my face and shown me who I am?'

'I will continue to stand in the tall grass, gazing up at your golden hair, for as long as you desire to call this place your home,' the troll replied. 'Just as I am certain our guest will return each night to the undergrowth at the edge of the clearing, listening to your song and to our conversations, never brave enough to show his face.'

'Guest?' Violet asked.

'Our words have been heard by another pair of ears tonight, and every night since I first desired to learn your name. A man, masquerading as a shadow.'

'Is there truly a man hiding in the forest, listening

to the most private words I've ever thought to speak aloud?'

'Quaking in his shiny boots—I can hear the foliage shivering. Come out here, little man, and face those you dared to overhear,' the troll commanded.

The prince, fragile fingers wrapped around his sword's unused hilt, shuffled into the moonlight beneath the overbearing tower. He turned his pale face towards Violet.

'What do you think you are doing here, loitering near my home?' Violet asked.

'The sound of your voice as you sang to the moon has brought warmth to my winter nights. Sitting beneath your tower was like stretching out before the hearth. I knew I should not be eavesdropping, but the stories shared between you and the troll, the cadence of your clever words, made it difficult to resist returning here each day just as the sun returns to the sea.'

'And yet you never chose to speak with me, or to return by light of day?'

'I regret my cowardice,' the prince replied. 'But I would happily return with the sunrise, simply to prove myself able.'

True to his word, the prince returned with the sun. He stood below Violet's tower and, his palms damp with terror and doubt, called up to the window. 'I stand before your tower now in the hope that you will forgive me for my shy silence.'

'I shall not forgive a man who knows so much of me and yet of whom I know so little.'

'I understand. If there is something you would

like to know of me, you need only ask. Though I hide myself from the view of most, I am an open book to you. If anyone deserves my honesty, it is she who I deceived for too many eves.'

'I have been told that names mean little, but what do you call yourself?'

'My name is Amir, and my title is prince.'

'Why do you hide yourself from the light, Prince Amir, as though burdened by the curse that the troll must carry?'

'I have many brothers and sisters, and I feel that I have little to offer when I stand beside them. They are each boisterous and clever, and just as I have grown in their shadow, I now live in the darkness of the forest and the moon.'

'You have the choice of seeing the world in all its beauty, basking in the daylight, and yet you squander it. I have never truly had that freedom, but if I had, I would not waste it,' Violet said.

'Perhaps that is true,' Amir replied. 'Or perhaps we are all trapped in some way, and trapped by ourselves. To an observer your prison is this tower, while mine is the palace, but I wonder if somewhere inside us we have the keys to these locks.'

'Perhaps.'

Amir continued to brave the sunlight and visited Violet each morning, while the troll returned each night. Violet slept little, her ongoing consciousness encouraged by the first bonds of friendship she had formed since she was forced from her village.

'Would you tell me about the palace?' Violet asked one day, beneath a cloudless midday sky.

'It is a place of too many rooms and too many people, contained within walls of stone built as high as your tower. The gardens are filled with fountains and flowers, the library overflows with hundreds of tales, and the kitchens have an endless supply of new delicacies that I have never tried.'

'It sounds wonderful,' Violet said.

'It is indeed a place of great beauty and yet, somehow, great loneliness.'

'This place, too, is one of incredible loneliness,' Violet replied. 'Though I barely know you better now than I did when you first revealed your face to me in the moonlight, each day I find myself excited for the dawn, as I know it brings with it your company.'

'I feel the same,' Amir said. 'How I wish you could come back to my palace with me so that I could show you its halls and you could fill them with wonder and conversation.'

'I think I would like that.'

Dusk approached, but the forest remained quiet. The birds circled the canopy, searching for the song they had lost. The troll worried that something dire had happened. She rushed from her bridge and crossed the forest with great strides, the branches quaking as the earth rattled beneath each step.

'What is the matter, my dear?' the troll asked when she arrived at the base of the tower, sharing the tall grass with Amir. 'Where is your magical song?'

'I have grown tired of the view from where I stand, for the world below is much wider than I could ever imagine. I thought that I was helping the world by staying here, but now I know that there are others like me. Perhaps those people need to see me—just as I needed to see you—to know that they are not alone. So, I am embarking on a journey.'

'And this is goodbye?' the troll asked.

'If you would like it to be. But, if you wish to come with me, you are welcome at the palace. Amir has spoken to his siblings and they have listened. Though they are extroverted and excitable, they are not wicked; they would love for you to join us there as often as you're able,' Violet replied.

'If you are as open with others as you have been with Violet, then I believe you could make an invaluable advisor to the royal family,' Amir said to the troll.

'Perhaps,' the troll replied, 'but if Violet truly does wish to leave her tower, have you considered how to free her from this spire without the aid of a door?'

Amir's face fell. 'No, I had not thought.'

The troll turned to Violet. 'Do you have anything in your room—like rope or sheets— that you could use to climb down from your prison?'

'Only one sheet, woven too thin to reach the ground or support my weight.'

'And I live beneath a bridge, with only the rocks to sleep upon,' the troll said. 'Do you have something that may aid our helpless friend?' she asked Amir.

'I am certain there are coils of rope stored in the palace stable by the blankets and the bridles. Perhaps I should return home, although that journey will take time.'

'I do not see another option,' the troll replied, 'so

I shall wait here until you return.'

'I am not helpless,' spoke Violet, her voice too close to the grass. 'Never mind your supplies—I have freed myself.'

Violet was dangling near the base of the tower. Her toes were curled, her feet not quite resting upon the ground. Her hands were clutching a golden plaited rope.

'I thought you said you had no rope,' Amir said.

'That's not rope,' the troll responded. 'I always knew your golden hair was long, but I never realised it could stretch the height of your tower.'

'Neither did I,' Violet responded. She touched the earth with one timid toe, before stepping into the grass. 'It has been so many years since I felt anything but timber and stone beneath my feet.'

Violet, Amir, and the troll arrived at the palace as the sun was rising. The troll was given a room with heavy curtains across the windows, and there she slept while Amir took Violet on a tour of the castle's many corridors. He offered her shoes, but she refused.

'I've lived here all my life,' Amir said, 'but I've never felt so at home within these walls as I do with you beside me.'

A room was prepared for Violet, but she rarely spent time there. Instead, she and Amir hid beneath the sheets in his bed, sharing hundreds of stories by torchlight. Some days, they went out exploring. On some occasions they left their adventures for the evenings so that the troll may accompany them.

The trio found this routine to be so agreeable

that Violet and Amir were married before the new year. She wore a short veil, simple combs tucked into her short tresses. After years of having heavy hair that dragged across the floor, Violet refused to grow it again, and Amir simply loved that she was happy.

Just beyond their one year anniversary, Violet gave birth to twins. The little boy was blond like his mother, and giggled before he cried; the little girl was dark-haired like her father, and was born wide-eyed, seeking the room's mysteries. He was named Sol, and she was named Lua.

Violet and Amir lived the rest of their days in the palace with their two children, Amir's many siblings, and the troll. They enjoyed a life of joy and heartbreak, success and compromise, until eventually their happy lives together ended, as they inevitably do.

Though Violet and Amir could not live eternally, their spirit fuelled the adventures of Sol and Lua—who sought their own happily ever afters—and in the troll, who left the palace to find a new forest and perhaps a new name.

6

CRYSTAL

I gathered my skirts and hid among the blankets folded in the back of the carriage. I listened until the quiet of the evening was broken by the delight of my stepsisters. Pearl and Margaret squeezed their gowns behind the carriage curtains, and my stepfather held the reins. Unknowingly, he took me to the royal masquerade ball.

When the carriage came to rest, I climbed down with light feet, crouching on the hoof-marked road as my stepfather said farewell to his daughters. 'Good luck, my girls,' he said, the moonlight reflected in his greedy eyes. 'Go and make us rich.' My hiding place departed and I was left curled on the gravel and mud, clutching my skirts.

My stepsisters climbed the stairs to the palace, too pleased with themselves to see me in the emptiness. I stood, looked at my masked reflection in my mud-streaked crystal shoes, and breathed in. I held the warm air against my heart, allowing it to fill me with bravery, before following my stepsisters inside.

The prince and the princess stood on a balcony overlooking the ballroom, where hundreds of hopeful guests hovered politely, brushing creases from their formal clothes and adjusting their masks. Some danced to the soft song of the string quartet, barely looking at their partners, thinking of nothing but dancing with the royal twins.

Once the prince and princess gracefully traced the path of the winding staircases and touched hands with their first dance partners, the tension of anticipation splintered. Conversations spread through the room, with guests chatting over miniature sandwiches or glasses of wine. I heard people laughing, and was reminded of how my stepfather's humour filled the rooms of my old house with frost and brambles. The sound felt like a lie, and it distanced me from the role that I wanted to learn how to perform.

I thought I could embed myself in these joyful conversations, and that such a crowd would come as a welcome relief from the cramped loneliness of the closet where I slept, but standing distanced from these people, all I could see were the masks they had layered upon their masks and I could not fathom how to belong in such a place. The scene before me felt incongruous to the fairy tales my stepsisters always told when they returned home from their ostentatious parties.

I escaped through an archway to the cool, perfumed breeze. I stood upon a terrace and overlooked a garden, which was touched gently by the moonlight, white light sprinkling the tips of leaves with late snow.

Footsteps shuffled across the shadows behind me.

'Is the ball not to your taste?' a young woman asked.

When I turned, I was met by the covered face of the princess. Momentarily, I was frozen by the imagined snowy chill, before I reminded myself to curtsey. My dress felt like rags with too few skirts when compared to the princess's gown.

'I'm sorry if you are not enjoying yourself,' she said. 'The ball was my brother's idea, but I've never been one for such extravagant events. I much prefer your idea of looking out across the garden, speaking truths to one another.'

'It's not that I do not like the ball, your highness,' I responded carefully, 'but simply that I am not accustomed to such an occasion.'

'How does a woman with such clever words and a stunning dress never see occasions such as these?' the princess asked.

'I am rarely permitted to leave my home,' I replied. 'Even tonight I locked the door to my bedroom and climbed down the railings by my window just to be here, admiring your garden.' 'You climbed down from your window in those delicate shoes? All the more reason to admire you.'

The string melodies quietened for a moment, revealing curious whispers that searched for the princess like the tendrils of a vine creeping up an abandoned wall of stone. 'It seems you are missed,' I said, as the music swelled once more.

'Please, would you accompany me inside? I would love to dance with somebody who would like to speak with me, rather than those guests who simply wish to distinguish the precise colour of my irises by staring at me so intensely that I fear they will fall to the ballroom floor, pulling me with them.'

I was led by a gentle but authoritative hand through the archway and across the floor. The princess guided me as we danced to the rhythm of strings and the muttering of guests. Others approached us and attempted to whisk the princess away from me, but she twirled me across the ballroom to avoid their grasp. The night dissolved like sugar crystals.

My eye came to rest upon the clock above the balcony, the ornate hands nearing midnight. 'I must soon depart, your highness,' I whispered.

'Why must you go so soon?'

'If I am to return home without my absence going noticed, I must ride upon my stepfather's carriage when he comes to collect my stepsisters at midnight. If not, I will be discovered and disowned.'

The princess spun her body around mine so that she could see the clock. 'And midnight draws close,' she said.

We danced across the floor, edging closer to the palace steps, and slipped away unnoticed. 'I must hide,' I said, 'so that my stepfather does not see me as he approaches.'

'Let me take your shoes so that you may run faster,' the princess suggested, 'then hide behind the hedges here. You will be able to climb onto the carriage unseen as he pauses on the road nearby.'

'Thank you, princess.'

'Though only my brother speaks my name, it is Lua. You may use it,' the princess said. 'Please, if you can climb through your window again tomorrow night, I would love to return these shoes to your callused feet and dance with you again on the second night of the royal ball.'

'I will try,' I replied, 'for I would love that also.'

My stepsisters told their excited stories over breakfast, and I swallowed my words. 'The prince danced with me twice,' Margaret said.

'And he danced with me three times!' Pearl countered.

'Even the princess danced with me once,' said Margaret, 'though I'm sure it was simply an accident. She couldn't possibly be one of *your* kind, stepsister.'

I stared into the mountains and valleys of my porridge.

'The princess disappeared at some point, anyway,' Pearl said, 'and, if she returned, I did not see her before we departed.'

My stepfather and stepsisters finished their meal before their conversation, and I excused myself to begin gathering the bowls and washing them in the tepid water in our sink.

'While I love to hear your stories, daughters,' my stepfather said, 'allow me to speak for a moment.' He turned his bristled face towards me. 'Girl, I noticed that the grains you brought back from the markets are mixed together in one pot. This evening, while your sisters are at the ball, you will separate them. You will make yourself useful to earn your keep in this house. I will not allow you to be as disrespectful as you were last night, locking yourself away in your room, alone with your spite.'

Though I knew I had returned with grains in separate sacks of cotton, I had no choice but to agree to my stepfather's demand.

That day, I cleaned the house with fervour, rushing through my chores so that I may begin sorting the grains while my stepsisters were still upstairs, sitting before their cracked mirrors. My nimble fingers scrambled through the clay pot, separating millet from maize.

I approached my stepfather before he could prepare the carriage. 'I have sorted the grains as you requested,' I said, 'but now I have taken quite ill. I found ash mixed in with the dry seeds, and breathing it into my lungs has left me with a cough that feels as though it may split my chest like the tree beneath the strike of lightning. I would like to rest, so that I may perform all of my chores for you again tomorrow.'

With reluctance, my stepfather agreed, and I was free to lock my bedroom door and run barefoot across the grass beneath my window.

Lua stole me from the foyer, a hand jutting out from behind a curtain and pulling me out of sight. 'You made it,' she said, our fingers intertwined.

'Have you hidden yourself behind this curtain all evening, waiting for me?'

'It was either that, or give false hope to guests for whom I care little, looking past them to the door while I longed for your arrival.'

With her words, birds were freed from their cages within my chest. 'Last night you shared your name with me, but the carriage arrived too quickly for me to share my own. Nowadays I am called many horrible things, but my mother named me Crystal.'

'Crystal,' Lua said, the word sparkling on her lips as though enchanted. 'Like your shoes.' She knelt before me in the cramped space and extended one of my shoes towards me. I pointed a bruised toe, and Lua slid the delicate crystal around my foot with more tenderness than I could remember experiencing in my life.

With my feet encased in transparency and Lua's fingers woven through mine again, we walked together into the ballroom. I was held close by this gentle woman who knew so little about me and yet accepted me completely, who energised me with her contagious smile. 'Why me?' I asked as we whirled.

'For so many people in this room, their mask is simply a reflection of their face. I can see past your mask and I know that there is not simply another behind it.'

Some guests reached out their hands and attempted to steal the princess as we danced, while others seemed not to recognise Lua in her new dress. It seemed most of the patrons were staring only at the prince, who had chosen a lady to lead across the floor.

When finally we lost our breath, Lua and I returned to the terrace where we first met, the hedges lighted by the moon once more. The prince followed us into the night, though we only noticed his presence once he spoke.

'My darling sister,' he said.

The ease I felt beside Lua dissipated, and I stood stiffly before the prince. Lua was overcome with no such discomfort. 'I have seen so little of you these last two days,' she said. 'Please, meet my beautiful companion, Crystal.' She reluctantly separated her fingers from mine, allowing my hand to be taken by the prince.

'A pleasure,' he said.

'Likewise, your highness,' I replied.

'Please, call me Sol. Such formality has always made me uneasy,' he said with a disarming smile as he released my hand. 'Sister, I would like you to meet a woman who I have quickly become infatuated with. This is Pearl.'

My stepsister.

Lua and Sol spoke for a few moments, about the house and the ball, while I tried not to stare at the woman who lived within my home and claimed I did not belong within it. Pearl was too fascinated by Sol's words to recognise me, laughing falsely at sentences not designed to be jokes, touching his arm endearingly at calculated moments. Though we were no longer in the ballroom, Pearl was performing a carefully choreographed dance.

'Enough of these cordialities,' Sol finally declared. 'We must return to the ballroom. I would like to dance with my love a hundred more times before the evening is over.'

Pearl allowed herself to be pulled inside.

'You were awfully quiet,' Lua said, returning her gaze to me. 'I hope you don't find my brother intimidating. He may be a prince by title, but mostly he's just a man.'

'That's not the reason for my discomfort,' I replied. 'The woman he stood beside is my stepsister.'

'Why did neither of you say?'

'I suppose she did not recognise me, for she has never seen me without my face streaked in dirt and my body draped in rags. She would not expect me to be in the gardens of the palace, holding the hand of a princess.'

'Dirt and rags?' Lua asked. 'I do not understand.'

Briefly, I wondered if Lua would still care for me if she knew my story.

'Before I was born, my father was sent to war,' I

said. 'He did not return, and my mother was forced to raise me alone. Struggling and starving, she married my stepfather when I was a child. Before she died, she told me tales of the pain he had caused her, of the atrocities she tolerated if only so that I could eat. My mother protected me from my stepfather, but after she was buried, there was nobody to stand between us. I am expected to do the chores that he forced upon my mother, as well as the chores he had always saved for me, while my stepsisters stand upon my back and chastise me. I am kept inside but for trips to the market. My stepfather and stepsisters say that I do not fit within this world, as the men I meet would be repulsed by me and no woman would ever share my unnatural attractions.'

'I am so sorry to hear what you have been through,' Lua said. 'But I am thankful that we share a trait deemed unnatural by your stepfather. It brings me joy to hear you speak so candidly, for I feared you may simply be dancing with me out of courtesy. How do you feel towards me?'

'When you hold my hand, I feel electricity pass between us that I have only read about in stories. And yet, this feeling is different from the stories too; I do not need to pretend to be something I am not for you.'

With curious fingers, Lua pulled my mask away from my eyes. 'You need only be yourself,' she said. To the faint melody of the string quartet and the whisper of the breeze through the garden, we shared our first kiss.

'Tomorrow,' Lua said, 'I would like to propose to you on the high balcony that overlooks the ballroom, and I would like every guest in the palace to see it. Do you think you might say yes?'

'I would love nothing more.'

Breakfast was tarnished by Margaret's tangible envy of her sister. 'Where did you disappear to last night?' she asked, her pursed lips pondering whether she truly desired the answer.

'The prince took me out onto the terrace, so that we could overlook the gardens,' Pearl told us. 'I met his sister, who is incredibly plain-looking. It is no wonder nobody has wanted to dance with her, and that she continues to hide from the guests in her chambers.'

'Perhaps the guests simply bore her,' I said.

'What would you know?' Pearl asked.

'I know more than you,' I replied.

I stood without asking to be excused and escaped to my bedroom before I could be captured. Within an old bag, I smuggled my mother's dresses, shoes, and tarnished photographs. I packed away her sewing machine and golden thread. I left behind my torn and dirty dresses, just as I left my torn and dirty family. Though the sun still floated high, I found solitude in the back of the carriage and waited for my stepsisters to appear with their curled hair and sequinned gowns.

The sun had barely touched the horizon when I overheard their conversations. 'Who cares that she has run away? I must be there early, for the prince declared that he would propose to me tonight,' Pearl said. 'Please be happy for me, sister.'

'I am happy for you,' Margaret replied, her words as false as every syllable Pearl had whispered to the prince.

'I am happy for us,' my stepfather said, gathering the reins and spurring on the horses.

I managed to escape the carriage with my belongings, unheard by my stepfather and unseen by my stepsisters. I stood in the empty entranceway, bags at my sides, and waited to be recognised. I peered behind the curtain, but Lua was not there.

When nobody appeared to greet me, I walked into the ballroom. It was void of guests, and even my stepsisters appeared to have gone elsewhere. I sought the comfort of the terrace, and here I found Lua gazing out upon the garden. She turned at the sound of my arrival.

'My love,' she said, 'you are here much earlier than I anticipated. I intended to greet you in the foyer—I hope the lonely walk through the rooms of the palace did not bother you.'

'I am familiar with loneliness.'

'You will soon struggle to remember the feeling,' Lua said. 'What have you brought with you?'

'These bags contain everything I own.'

'Then let us take them upstairs and find you a place to belong.' She shared the burden of my possessions and led me through the palace. We passed spaces as large as the house I had abandoned and, while we navigated this labyrinth that I doubted I could ever navigate alone, we heard a conversation grow louder through the walls.

'What do you know of my stepsister?' Pearl screeched, shards of wicked glass catching in her throat.

'Today I have heard tales of how you and your family treat her. I cannot love somebody who acts so cruelly towards another,' Sol replied.

I turned to Lua, and was met with a finger to my lips.

'If you knew what she is, then you would know that she deserves it,' Pearl retorted.

'I know enough,' Sol said. 'I know that she was locked away for her attraction to men and women, an identity shared by my sister and my late mother, the queen. My mother used to tell us stories of how she was once trapped in a tower by her father's words, losing her first love and her home, because she was queer. She often reminded us that she would never abandon us, no matter who we are and who we love. I cannot care for someone who treats another as my mother was once treated.'

'But we were to be married,' Pearl whimpered.

'We were, and now we are not. I expect both of you to leave the palace immediately, before I call the guards.'

My stepsisters passed me in the hallway, the masks pulled from their faces.

Sol raised a hand and the string quartet was silenced. The guests turned their heads towards the balcony, towards the prince, the princess, and me.

'My cherished subjects, my guests,' he began. 'Tonight is the third eve of our splendid ball, which was held as an opportunity for myself and my sister to meet all of you and, if we were lucky, find love. I thought I had succeeded, but it is with great discontent that I must announce that I was mistaken. Thankfully, my sister has much better taste than I.'

Sol gestured to Lua, encouraging her to stand before their guests and speak.

'Good evening,' she began, her voice laced with unfamiliar formality. 'I hope that you are enjoying the third and final night of the royal ball. I know I have spent little time speaking with each of you individually, so now I would like to speak to you all and hopefully explain my absence.

'I have had the pleasure of hosting many events such as this in my time as princess, and the joy of attending many more. I have met so many people, but alongside me now stands the most courageous and interesting person I have ever met. And tonight, with all of you before us, I would like to ask her to marry me.'

Lua knelt, this time clutching a ring in place of a shoe. 'Crystal, would you be my wife?'

'I would be honoured,' I replied.

We kissed to a cacophony of echoing applause.

7
SILVER

I fell from my world into one just as dark and just as cold. I raised shivering palms to my face, but it remained unchanged. I gathered my rags and scarves around my hideous form and set off along unknown streets, avoiding the unavoidable glares of disgusted passers-by.

I had no destination in mind, for I had no idea where I was, let alone where I could be going. I allowed myself to be carried by the street, like the current of a river, wondering if these bodies were propelling me towards a perilous drop.

This world could be a reflection of the one I left, with its monochrome cold. The skeletal trees had been replaced by buildings resembling tombstones. People walked briskly to avoid considering their grief.

Buffeted by the cold of the people and the snow, a little girl shivered on the side of the street. Her feet were the same red and blue of my own, the frost marking our skin. Her face was smudged like a newspaper left out in the rain.

She held out a handful of matches, her lips moving around sounds that remained out of my reach. The thrum of people sneered at her like she was inconveniencing them. As I neared her, she turned the matches towards me.

'A match for a coin?' she asked, her voice husky.

'I have no coins, or else I'd give you them all. My shoes too, if my feet weren't as bare as your own,' I replied.

'No coins at all? Not even those lovely silver ones, that you can polish against your apron until they shine bright enough to see your face in?'

'No coins at all.' I lowered my scarf from my face, unwrapping its length. 'But I do have this scarf. It will help keep you warm.'

'I know you,' the little girl said as she let me wrap the scarf around her neck and shoulders. She reached into her apron and removed a photograph, the same one I had seen hanging from the darkroom ceiling the day I fled the house.

'Who gave this to you?' I asked.

'A woman with no name.'

'What did she look like?'

'All hardness and softness, terror and kindness, and sometimes flickering as though she was not truly here at all. She had boxes of photographs printed with darkness and light, and I asked for this image of a face because it reminded me of my own.'

'And she just gave it to you?'

'For a match.'

'When was this?'

'Three winters ago.'

'But this photograph was drying in my darkroom only this morning.'

'Then it must have been a long day.'

I wondered if it were my love who passed through this place, for who else could have carried my portrait with them through the snow? And if three years had passed since she walked the streets of this city, how many had passed before that? How many lifetimes had my love lived, wandering the worlds through doorways I had opened, losing the name I once knew her by?

Was she looking for me? Or had she given this portrait away for a match because she was tired of carrying the burden of my face? Was she pleased to be finally rid of me?

I would have posed these questions to the little girl, certain she lacked the answers, but she was being propelled downstream again by faceless crowds that stretched to the horizon. I joined the river too, and let it take me to where everybody else was going, wondering if my love might be there.

8
GUILT

Strings of photographs adorned the market stall awning, their light and shadow stark away from the sunset colours of the safelight. More photographs spilled from boxes stacked across the stained tablecloth, and more still were squeezed into blistering frames.

I wasn't sure how much time had passed. I had displayed my photographs in the markets of so many lands, where the forgotten always congregate like patrons worshipping freedom. I hoped that the hordes might bring Innocence to me, or else someone might see her face among the photographs of trees and houses, and tell me where to find her. The stalls always looked the same, and so did the faces that peered into photographs as though they saw reflections of themselves.

I often wondered if I had done the right thing, leaving home. Perhaps if I had just stayed there as the snow thawed, Innocence would have returned on her own. Maybe Innocence was already back, taking photographs of branches laden with new life, wondering where I had disappeared to for the long years in between. I felt guilty when I thought of her, in our darkroom, developing photographs alone.

My heart searched the colours of the spaces I visited, and yet was always drawn back towards that darkroom. I had never longed to settle before I met Innocence, but she wished to make a home, and so I stopped my constant wandering and found comfort in her desire. But now I was running again, wondering if that certainty and stillness could be returned to me.

I heard whispers by my market stall, of ogres fleeing the mountain caves. Others called them giants, and some trolls, like these foreign creatures had no names of their own. I had never met anybody who quite resembled me, and yet the same whispers called me the troll with the photographs, and I couldn't help wondering if there were creatures like me being forced to wander a world away from their homes.

Under the pretence of asking these displaced trolls if they had seen Innocence on their travels, I took my boxes of photographs and the coins for which I sold these impressions of the world, and began a journey towards the war. I did not know how long the walk would take, but it mattered little, for I had nowhere else to be, and nowhere else to go.

9

STERLING

I stood beside the river of people, holding my bouquet of matches out to the crowd. 'A match for a coin? A match for a coin?' I said. Once I shouted the phrase, but too many days in the cold had stolen my voice.

One passer-by knocked the matches from my hand and they scattered across the snow. I knelt and gathered them up again, wet circles marking the front of my apron. I shivered.

'Where are your shoes little girl?' a woman asked.

'I lost them,' I replied, but she was not looking for an answer, continuing on her way. My shoes had fallen off as I rushed across a road: one was squashed by a speeding taxi while the other was picked up by a homeless boy, who ran into the night with it. I had little desire to chase him; my father's hand-me-downs would likely have fitted him better in any case.

I considered returning to my parents after that and begging for another pair, but I hadn't sold a single match this winter and I knew that without coins, I would not be welcome. I was hardly welcome even if I carried a purse that could buy us bread and wine for Christmas.

Another person who had lost their shoes stopped at the road beside me.

'A match for a coin?' I asked.

'I have no coins, or else I'd give you them all. My shoes too, if my feet weren't as bare as your own,' the woman who owned the feet replied.

'No coins at all? Not even those lovely silver ones, that you can polish against your apron until they shine bright enough to see your face in?'

'No coins at all.'

The woman lowered her scarf and I recognised her. She extended the scarf to me as I reached into my apron pocket.

'I know you,' I said, extending the photograph of a Snow Queen that I carried with me.

'Who gave this to you?'

'A woman with no name.'

'What did she look like?'

I tried to remember the face of the woman, the image morphing in my memory. 'All hardness and softness, terror and kindness, and sometimes flickering as though she was not truly here at all. She had boxes of photographs printed with darkness and light, and I asked for this image of a face because it reminded me of my own.'

'And she just gave it to you?'

'For a match.'

'When was this?'

I paused, counting on frozen fingers. 'Three winters ago.'

'But this photograph was drying in my darkroom, only this morning.'

'Then it must have been a long day.'

The Snow Queen was beautiful and frightening, all straight lines and sharp angles. Questions danced behind her eyes, but I didn't have time to help her search for answers. Instead, I hurried back onto the street, recommencing my own search for coins.

Though the Snow Queen gave me her scarf, it offered little warmth. I found a place between the buildings where the wind could find less of my exposed skin. I watched people in their coats and shoes pass by the entrance to the alleyway, and longed for either. The fabric of my apron was soaked by the flurries of snow and slush that crowded the corner.

I held out the matches, examining them, their bodies like a cluster of limbless, red-faced dolls. I struck one against the brick. Once, twice. It took a few attempts to catch, and fizzled in the damp. I threw it aside.

I struck another match on a square of wall that had been shielded from the snow by a metal bin. It flared and hissed, and orange washed over me, like the light of a fireplace. I had seen a fireplace once, in the common area of the city library. I visited with my class, back when I attended school. As I watched the flicker of the match, I was back there.

My teacher asked me to sit at the front of the class and read from a picture book she'd chosen from the rows of shelves. The fire warmed my back, and made the pages feel dry and crinkly. Although I liked to read, I preferred telling my own stories, so while the teacher wasn't listening, I took my friends on journeys of my own making.

My classmates and I walked the streets of the city, explored enchanted forests, and visited the stars.

The match burnt out. I turned the misshapen splinter over, crushing the ash and coating my fingerprints in darkness. I struck another and new shapes danced in the light.

I sat at a long table in a hall adorned with tinsel. My place was set with a red and green cloth napkin, a Christmas cracker, a knife and fork, and a ceramic plate with holly leaves and berries painted around its edges. Faces I did not recognise surrounded me, their smiles filled with perfect, white teeth.

Arms passed food across the table and hands served salads and meats onto plates. I ate roast chicken, smoked ham, and baked potatoes.

A boy grasped my fingers beneath the table, beneath a napkin, beneath his sly smile.

Stretching my memories, the match's warmth showed me scenes that had never happened, where I was older and warmer and filled with joy. Desperate for more stories such as this, I let another match burst into flame.

I was in the gym of a school I'd never seen before, Christmas lights blinking from the ceiling. I stood by a doorway with a girl I didn't know, her hand on my arm. 'You know that photograph that you carry?' she asked.

'What about it?'

'Who is it?'

'The Snow Queen.'

The girl laughed Christmas bells and cinnamon. 'But who is it really?'

I shook my head and she pouted.

'Well, if you're not going to talk, at least do something else with those lips,' she said, pointing up to the little cluster of mistletoe hanging above us.

Each match's flame was fleeting, and I longed to feel the kindness of these unknown faces for more than just a moment. Desperate, I took the handful of matches and struck it against the bricks so that it burst into a rose of red and orange and white. The dark and cold of the alleyway was suffocated by the brightness, and in the glow I saw so many hands reaching out to me, open and beckoning.

I let myself be carried by their love into the light.

10
TABBY

My sister once told me that she was the stream and that I was the brushfire. She called me wild, like the tabby cat who once lived in the palace gardens, who fed from my palms but nipped at her heels. I suppose I was always different from her.

When I turned sixteen, I ran away. She was the only one I told, but I don't think she believed I would truly leave. 'You may be wild, but you are not foolish,' Olive said. I haven't seen her since.

In the country, I met a miller. He gave me shelter and I worked for my keep alongside his two selfish sons. There I passed several years, and I was happy enough, until the miller died.

'What do you mean he gave me to you in his will?' I asked.

'Look,' Coy replied, brandishing a piece of paper. 'Your signature is scratched across the bottom of this contract, and my father passed this contract on to me.'

'I am not an object to be passed down a lineage,'

I said, snatching the contract. 'And what do you intend to do with me? I work in the mill, but your brother owns the mill now.'

'I am yet to decide,' Coy replied, 'but my brother has offered us a place here until I find my own home and my own way. Once I know my calling, you will follow me across the countryside.'

'I've never followed anyone and I'm not about to start,' I argued, but Coy cared little for my retort.

'Perhaps one day I will make you my wife,' he said, certain of his ownership, before leaving me standing alone in the common area.

It was not that I found the idea of marriage unappealing, but I had no interest in tethering myself to either of the young men with whom I shared the mill; if I did have such an intent, I would have mentioned it years before. I considered leaving the mill and moving on, returning to the nomadic life I chose when I fled the palace. When I was younger, crossing the many kingdoms until I walked unrecognised was an adventure, but I had grown to enjoy the particular mud that gathered beneath my fingernails at the mill; I resolved to continue toiling there until the brothers parted ways.

It soon became apparent that Coy found working for his brother, Archibald, more difficult than following the orders of their father. In return for our work, Archibald granted us shelter and food, but Coy longed for more.

One night, as I read by lamplight, Coy confronted Archibald about the perceived injustice. The argument carried through the timber floor like heavy rain on the old roof.

'I should be given wealth for my work here. I work as much as you, and yet you keep the coins we are paid for our produce and I am given nothing.'

'You should be grateful for the bed you sleep in and the food you eat. Your work is of such low quality that you should scarcely be paid at all, let alone granted more than you are given. When we worked for Father, we did so because we were told to and we had nowhere else to go; if you have somewhere else to be, you are welcome to leave the mill that is rightfully mine.'

But of course, Coy had nowhere to go but his bedroom, in which he locked himself for several days. For his lack of work, Coy was given less, and so he stole from my plate.

I had travelled the paths that traced their way through fields and forests many times in the years I lived at the mill, hauling our grains and flours to the market squares of nearby villages and returning with little bags of silver and gold. I began to follow these paths at dusk, seeking some way of sating my rumbling stomach.

I had often been pursued during my travels to the villages, with women attracted to my strength and men to my servitude. With marriage unnecessary, I allowed myself to be fussier than my father would ever have permitted; I wondered now if perhaps partnership would solve my present issue of hunger and my future concerns of homelessness.

One evening I found a rabbit warren and approached it with a flour sack filled with broken stems and torn leaves from our stripped vegetable garden. I laced the grass with temptation and waited for a naïve rabbit to surface. I caught it in the sack and swiftly broke its neck; with it broke all thought that marriage might hold a necessary solution.

I built a fire by the path and cooked the rabbit, not wishing to have the meat snatched at the mill. Above the trees, I could see flickering lights filling the windows of a palace that resembled the one in which I was born. I wondered if the ruler of this kingdom knew of a royal family from a faraway land who had lost a daughter to the night.

Once I had eaten, I returned to the mill. The brothers would not speak to one another, a fissure continuing to grow between them. It seemed that a separation between the brothers would arise sooner than I had anticipated, and I knew that it was time to prepare for my departure.

The following dusk, I returned to the rabbit warren. I caught two and cooked one atop the fire. I ate my first meal of the day while I sat cross-legged in the grass, and I carried the second body through the forest to the palace. On the steps, I encountered two guards.

'I seek an audience with the king on behalf of the Marquis de Carabas,' I announced with urgency, recalling the convincing royal persona I once taught myself to embody.

They led me through the halls to the throne room, where I waited on the purple carpet and attempted to brush the patches of mud from my dress. Another guard looked at me uncertainly, but ushered me into the throne room when I assured him of the gift I sought to offer the king.

His majesty was seated upon a golden chair, polished so that I could see myself in its curves. It reminded me of another life. I curtseyed and waited to be spoken to.

'Good evening, young woman. I have been informed that you are here on behalf of your ruler.'

'I have brought a simple offering from the Marquis de Carabas to bequeath to you.'

'Carabas? I have never heard of such a place.'

'My ruler was concerned that this may be the case, for although his land borders yours, he rarely leaves his territory or converses with his neighbours. This gift is an apology as much as an overdue greeting.'

'You may return to your ruler and inform him that his gift is appreciated,' the king declared.

'Thank you, your majesty.'

I left with empty hands and concerns that my plan, so carefully devised, may not find success.

The following dusk, as I walked to the warren, I stumbled across a pond in the forest. There, flipping droplets of water from their wings, gathered a group of ducks. Wishing not to hunt all of the rabbits, that evening I caught two of the wild birds and brought one before the throne.

'Your majesty,' I said with a curtsey, 'I have returned with another gift from the Marquis de Carabas.'

'The generosity of the marquis is appreciated,' the king replied. 'Allow me to grant you a small token for you to return to your ruler as a mark of my gratitude.'

The king sent me into the night with a bag of silver coins—heavier than any handful of coins I had ever carried back from the markets. The metal reflected my likeness a hundred times, and I hid the many mirrors beneath my bed.

This became a familiar routine: I would harden the callouses across my palms as I worked for Archibald at the mill; I would walk at dusk and hunt for my dinner and for the king; I would arrive at the palace with offerings from the imagined marquis; and I would smuggle my newfound riches back into the mill as I prepared for my eventual, necessary escape.

One evening, when I arrived at the palace with a basket of freshly caught fish, I interrupted a discussion between the king and a woman who I assumed was his daughter. The king had determined that it was time for the princess to seek a husband, so that the king may expand his reach to another of the many lands bordering his kingdom.

The princess hesitated in the doorway before she slinked past me; I saw something familiar in her eyes.

The king cared little about what I had overheard, immediately turning his attention to the gifts I had brought. 'The Marquis de Carabas is a remarkable hunter and skilled fisherman, and I simply must meet him. I will arrange for a banquet that the marquis may attend as our guest of honour at his earliest convenience.'

'The marquis would happily meet with you as soon as you are available, your majesty,' I said, with no idea how to arrange such a thing. 'Tomorrow night, perhaps?'

'Tomorrow I ride through the kingdom with my

daughter, as is our tradition, but two nights from now I will ensure he is treated splendidly.'

'I will inform him immediately.'

Unable to sleep, I commenced work before the dawn, watching the waterwheel as thoughts turned in my mind. I was struggling to find a solution to my predicament, and I wondered if I must simply stop visiting the king before my deceit was discovered.

My contemplation was interrupted when Coy approached. 'Where have you been disappearing to?' he asked.

'I'm sorry?'

'The night before last I checked your room, the common area, and the fields, but you were a ghost. Last night I watched you leave the mill with the final sliver of the sun.'

'I spend my evenings walking through the forest or along the stream.'

'With a flour sack of scraps or a coil of fishing line?' he asked. 'You are not walking to enjoy the scenery; you are going out to hunt. Why do you never return with meat and fish to share?'

The waterwheel turned behind Coy's shoulder and the pieces of a plan fell into place as I replied. 'You are right—I have been hunting—but only to bring gifts to the king. You see, I have a way for you to leave the mill and seek freedom from the orders of your brother.'

Coy's suspicion remained evident in the curve of his eyebrows and the tightness of his jaw, and yet curiosity bested him. 'What do you have in mind?'

'If you listen to me and do precisely as I say, I

promise you will be able to live as you please,' I said. 'Meet me by the gate this afternoon and you will see.'

I led Coy into the forest, my newfound wealth a heavy secret, wrapped in a flour sack and weighing down my pockets. The stream traced a line between the trees, and the towers of the palace overlooked the rocks where we paused. 'Remove your clothes and bathe here,' I said.

'Remove my clothes?' Coy asked. 'How the heck will this help me be free of the mill?'

'Trust me.'

With uncertain fingers, Coy unbuttoned his dusty shirt and took off his torn trousers; he draped them across the rocks before wading into the water. While Coy bathed, I hid his clothes in the nearby bushes, camouflaged by the undergrowth.

'How long do I need to swim here?'

'Be patient,' I replied.

I could hear the sound of hooves following the trail that ran the length of the stream. I rushed to the roadside and waved at the driver. 'Halt,' I called.

The horses slowed and the carriage stopped. 'What is the meaning of this?' the driver asked.

'My ruler—the Marquis de Carabas—was bathing in the stream when a gang of thieves passed by and stole his clothes,' I said. 'Please, would you help us?'

The carriage door opened with the king's familiar voice. 'The Marquis de Carabas, you say?'

'He sought to enjoy the afternoon light and the temperate water, but now his day has been ruined.'

'This simply won't do,' the king declared. 'Tell the marquis that one of my travelling party will return to the palace immediately to fetch our finest clothes and softest towels.'

When I returned to the stream, I found an embarrassed Coy, his arms folded across his body as he waded by the bank. 'Where have you been?' he asked.

'Speaking with the king.'

'I tried to follow you, but my clothes are gone.'

'Soon the king will offer you new clothes and refer to you as the Marquis de Carabas, and you must play that role.'

'What's a marquis?'

One of the king's assistants soon returned, averting his eyes as Coy draped himself in royal robes. The assistant led Coy to the king's carriage, where he was greeted cordially. 'The Marquis de Carabas, whom I have heard so much about—at last, we meet! Please, join me in my carriage and ride with me and my daughter.'

'With pleasure, your majesty,' Coy responded, stepping up to take his place alongside the royal family.

I walked well ahead of the meandering carriage as it rolled through the forest. The carriage was restrained by the forest path, but I took shortcuts through the trees. We were headed towards an edge of the forest I had never seen and that denoted the boundary of this kingdom.

In the fields beyond the forest, I encountered a group of farmers working frantically to scythe the wheat. I paused among them. 'Who owns this land?' I asked.

'The ogre and the troll,' the group replied, their voices shaking at the thought of the terrifying beasts.

Once, as I stood with bags of flours and grains in the market of a village near the mill, I heard rumours of an ogre and a troll who ruled a land that bordered on the kingdom we inhabited. It was said that the pair harboured great magic and were able to shapeshift into any creature they wished. 'The ogre has lived for centuries,' the villagers had whispered, 'and the troll for longer still.'

'Have they always lived here, so close to where we toil our land and bake our bread?' someone had asked.

'They have been here for generations,' somebody else responded, 'but once upon a time, before the war drove him away, the ogre lived in the mountain caves.'

'And the troll?'

'Some say she lived at the edge of the world,' the villager replied, 'while others say she lived in a different world entirely.'

'You must leave,' the farmers said as I observed their panicked slashing, 'for if you are found here, we will lose our jobs or our lives, and our families will perish without us.'

I took a handful of silver coins from the flour sack in my pocket, hopeful that if my plan succeeded, I would soon have even more wealth for my escape. I offered the coins to the farmers. 'Take these and, with them, feed your families,' I said. 'The king will be passing through here in a moment. When he asks you who owns these lands, tell him these farms are the property of the esteemed Marquis de Carabas. Do not fear the ogre and the troll; just as I have provided for you now, I will protect you from their wrath.'

'What could you possibly do, a young woman like

you?' the farmers asked. But they took my coins and gave their word.

When the carriage arrived in the fields and the king saw the farmers, he halted the driver and called from the carriage window. 'You there, who owns these lands?'

'These farms are owned by the Marquis de Carabas,' the farmers replied.

The king looked impressed. He turned to Coy and spoke words I could not hear as the carriage began rolling again, restricted by the paths that wound through the fields. I rushed ahead, dashing through the wheat.

Soon the paths turned to cobblestones, and they led me to the gates of a looming manor. On the road was an ornate carriage, and by it stood a driver and a handful of servants, whom I approached. 'Who owns this carriage?' I asked.

'The ogre and the troll,' they replied.

I took a handful of gold coins from the flour sack and offered them to the driver and servants. 'Take these and, with them, feed your families,' I said. 'The king will be arriving in a moment. When he asks you who owns this carriage, tell him it is the property of the esteemed Marquis de Carabas. Do not fear the ogre and the troll; just as I have provided for you now, I will protect you from their wrath.'

'You must take care, for even speaking such a threat will surely be the death of you,' the driver said. But he and the servants took my coins and gave their word. With the key on his brass keyring, the driver opened the gate. As I neared the manor, I heard the carriage approaching.

The manor door was unlocked and in the hallway stood a butler, speaking with the house staff. 'Is this manor owned by the ogre and the troll?'

'The manor was once owned by the ferocious pair, but only the ogre remains.'

'Was the troll killed?'

The butler laughed. 'The troll cannot die,' he replied, 'but she does not know how to own a house. Eternally restless, she has commenced a new journey.'

'And the ogre?'

'In the drawing room. Though I would not go in there, if I were you; he will surely kill you for being here and then us for letting you pass.'

I took a handful of gemstones from the flour sack and offered them to the butler and house staff. 'Take these and, with them, feed your families,' I said. 'The king will be entering the manor in a moment. When he asks you who owns these halls, tell him every inch of this magnificent home is the property of the esteemed Marquis de Carabas. Do not fear the ogre; just as I have provided for you now, I will protect you from his wrath.'

'If you have made it this far, then I know better than to attempt to discourage you from doing the impossible,' the butler said. He and the house staff took my gemstones and gave their word.

I found the ogre sitting in the drawing room, pondering the fireplace. 'Ogre?' I called.

'Who let you into my manor?'

'I let myself in,' I replied.

'I suppose I am not surprised that a woman who speaks so calmly to an ogre simply let herself into his manor. What do you want from me?'

'I heard that you know how to shapeshift,' I said. 'I want to know if it's true.'

The ogre's laugh thudded onto the stone, the sound of bones breaking. 'Of course it is true.'

'Could you prove it to me?'

The ogre transformed into a lion, only his matte black eyes remaining unchanged. The lion leapt atop the nearest table and roared; my body quaked, but I stood my ground and feigned indifference.

When the ogre turned back, I tried to seem bored. 'A lion?' I asked. 'I have seen creatures transform into lions before. Becoming the largest and most terrifying of creatures when you yourself are large and terrifying must be easy. What I scarcely believe is the rumour that you can become the smallest and sweetest of animals. I must admit that I think this is quite impossible.'

'I can transform into anything, no matter the size!' the ogre declared, before transforming into a rabbit. I caught the rabbit in the flour sack from my pocket and swiftly broke its neck.

The king entered the drawing room, led by the timid butler and trailed by the princess and Coy. 'Your manor is simply marvellous,' the king said.

'Your kindness is appreciated,' Coy replied.

'And your staff are so quick to declare their loyalty to you,' the king added. 'Your carriage is ornate and sturdy, and your fields are wide and bountiful. I would love your land to be joined with mine— would you consider proposing to my daughter, Princess Saara?'

'Your daughter is beautiful and I would love for her to be made my wife,' Coy replied. 'Then it is settled,' the king declared. 'We shall arrange for a feast.'

I cared little for the politics of royalty, and wondered only if this new arrangement would grant me the wealth I desired to begin my journey elsewhere. Though, when Princess Saara interrupted the dealings with her thoughts on the matter, my own musings quieted.

'I will not marry this man,' she declared.

'It is not up to you,' the king said.

'Of course it is, for you can only marry me to someone if I choose to stand before your altar,' Saara replied. She turned to me. 'I have watched from my window as you kill rabbits with your bare hands and roast them for yourself atop the fire. I know that this man is not a marquis, and that you are much more than you say. You possess too much wit to be a simple servant. Tell me, who are you?'

'Many years ago I was more than who I am now, but in this place I am simply Tabby,' I replied.

'Well, Tabby, if that is all you wish to share, then I am willing to accept it. But what I will not accept is being married to a man I hardly know. I am bored by his simplicity, and it is a trait typical of the men who fill the halls of the palace and who court me with the subtly of an earthquake. Let him have this land that I know you claimed for him, but let me have you.'

'Me? What do you want with me?'

'Well, if my father so desires that I marry, then I long to marry you.'

A strangled sound from the king's throat suggested he disagreed, but he did not speak. Coy also stood silently, the oversized royal robes dripping from his limbs like candle wax. The scene was paused, awaiting my response, a spotlight trained upon my wasted features.

'I have lived within the confines of castles and palaces for too many years already,' I said. 'I have learnt to escape royalty and I do not wish to return to it.'

'Good,' Saara replied. 'Perhaps you can teach me.'

11

CORAL

Coral rested in the secluded cove, her torso stretched across the sand and her tail swaying beneath the turquoise water. Many months had passed since she had found a small wooden chest on the ocean floor and now it sat open, half-buried in the sand. The decaying timber was filled with hundreds of stories, some incomplete or damaged, some written in languages she was yet to teach herself, and some overflowing with drawings of places and objects Coral struggled to believe could be real. Her damp hands distorted the pages of the leather volume she was clutching.

Between the covers was written the story of a princess who, after being rescued by a prince, ran away with him to his castle and lived happily ever after. 'Happily ever after' were words Coral learnt quickly, comparing the phrase between several of the books she had collected. The pictures on those pages always looked similar: a prince, a princess, and a beautiful castle. And all of the characters always seemed to have legs.

Through the canopy of palm fronds, streaks of colour were beginning to creep into the vibrant blue. Coral returned the book to her collection, tucking it in among the other trinkets that the chest contained: a piece of mirror, a hairbrush, a spinning top. She closed the chest and covered it with sand and leaves.

Her tail caught the sunset light of pink and gold as Coral crossed the reef in search of open water. Once the sand fell away into the ocean, she dived towards the depths and her tail turned the dull grey of driftwood once again.

Every day at dusk, Coral met Chelle at her home on the far side of the city, where Coral told stories of the surface. That afternoon, after Coral had described the colours of the sky and warmth of the sunlight, Chelle asked, 'Would you tell me another of your tales?'

Chelle had heard all of Coral's stories before, translated and memorised from the pages of her leather-bound books, but Chelle never seemed to tire of the same stories of trickery and true love, so Coral told the tales again and again.

Once upon a time there lived a queen and a king who longed for a child. When they were blessed with a beautiful daughter, they invited all of the kind, wise women in the kingdom to the celebrations. Each of the women gifted the young princess with good fortune, to ensure she would live a happy, perfect life, but before the last wise woman could approach the child, an aged fairy entered the room. Though the fairy was known to be very wise and very powerful, nobody had wanted to invite her, for they were scared of her magic. Filled with bitterness, the fairy cursed the princess so that she might die in her eighteenth year after pricking her finger on a sea urchin.

Thankfully, the last of the wise women still had not granted the child a gift. Unable to counter the powerful curse entirely, the woman ensured that the sea urchin would not kill the young princess, but would simply send her into a deep sleep, to be lifted only by the kiss of a prince.

'I love this one,' Chelle said. 'I wish I could go to the surface.'

'You can,' Coral replied. 'I always invite you.'

'I don't mean I want to lie on the beach with our tails in the water; I want to be in one of these stories with you. You know, happily ever after.'

'But happily ever after is for a princess and a prince who have a castle and legs,' Coral said. 'It's not for us.'

'At the very least, you are a princess,' Chelle said. 'You're one tail-swish closer than I am.'

It was late when Coral returned to the palace of the Sea King and entered the grounds where all of her sisters gathered, tending to their gardens while their grandmother observed. Each of the Sea Princesses was granted their own portion of the seabed to do with as they wished.

Most of the sisters nurtured corals and anemones, these gently swaying bodies gathered around a selection of strange objects that had fallen from the surface; when they were not tending to their gardens, the sisters swam into the surrounding water in search of new treasures that may have plummeted to the ocean floor.

'Where have you been?' Coral's grandmother asked.

'I have been trawling through the sand in search of trinkets for my garden,' Coral replied.

'Don't lie to your grandmother,' her father chastised, appearing through the palace doors. 'When are you going to bring the woman who has captured your attention to the castle so that we might meet her?'

Coral's face filled with colour. 'It's not like that,' she said, thinking of the happily ever after she longed for. 'It can't be.'

The Sea Princesses each had their own room, and Coral escaped to hers. She curled her tail beneath her body and went in search of dreams about weddings on the surface, her face bathed in the sunlight and her toes sinking in the sand.

Legs and feet followed Coral into waking and, for a moment, she felt trapped by her tail, as though somebody had bound her limbs. Her panic was soon replaced by familiar disappointment; although she loved her tail, she felt it impossible to find happiness in the ocean.

Coral left the palace before her sisters had risen. Her father was not loitering in the foyer and her grandmother had yet to enter the gardens, so her passage was uncontested. She longed to bathe in the sunshine of the secluded cove again that morning, but her dull grey tail carried her elsewhere: away from the palace, away from the bustling city that surrounded it and into the canyon that marked the edge of the Sea King's dominion. There, cut from one of the steep walls like the bite of a gigantic shark, was a cave. Within the cave lived the Sea Witch.

Everybody in the ocean knew of the Sea Witch, but no one went to speak with her. The ferocity of her powers was well known, with stories passed down through generations, and so she was avoided like the aged fairy in Coral's favourite fairy tale.

Coral paused by the entrance to the cave. The canyon was filled with crushing shadows, darker than anywhere she had ever explored, and the cave was darker still.

'Why are you here, my dear?' said a voice from within the blackness. 'Don't you know that it's dangerous to visit the Sea Witch?'

'My father also tells me that it's dangerous to swim to the surface, and yet I bask in the sun every day.'

'You're a fool,' the Sea Witch said.

'Maybe.'

'What do you want?'

'My own happily ever after,' Coral replied, still hovering over the threshold.

'And what do you need for this to be your reality?'

'A prince, a castle, and a pair of legs.'

The Sea Witch laughed. 'You have spent too many days reading the stories of the surface, and now you wish to live there. Let me tell you—I lived on the surface once, many years ago, but I lost my love above the waves and I am yet to find solace below them. Sky or sea, there is no guarantee of happiness.'

'But the princesses in those stories smile so beautifully as they stand in their castles with their true loves. Their fingers are always entwined with those of a prince and they always have legs; they never have tails.'

'And you want to fall into one of these stories, to fall in love? You do not think love is possible here, in the ocean you have known all your life? If you truly want to abandon your life here so that you can dance on the sand, I will help you.'

'You will?'

'I am of my word,' the Sea Witch replied. 'But as payment for my service, you must do something for me.'

'Anything.'

'Since you love stories so much, you must listen to one of my own, from before I lived invisible in the darkness of my sea cave. Come inside, my dear, and make yourself comfortable on the stone.'

Coral followed the voice into the shadows, able to see only impressions through the gloom. The outline of a woman sat upon an embankment, and curled beneath her like tentacles were two muscular legs. The story started like sandpaper, constructed from words that had sat within a throat for too long.

Once upon a time, as that is how all stories must begin, there lived a queen and a king who longed for a child.

12

HAZEL

The royal family was granted a blessing in the form of a beautiful daughter, and all of the kind, wise women in the kingdom were invited to the celebrations. I watched the wise women gift the young princess with good fortune, each of them hoping the child would live a happy, perfect life.

Before I could share my own wisdom with the child, an old and haggard fairy entered the room. We had thought of the fairy, but had not wished to invite her; she had used her powers for great evil before and we did not wish to put the young princess's life at risk. Her throat filled with bitter, tarnished reflections of the world surrounding her, and the fairy cursed the princess so that she might die in her eighteenth year after pricking her finger on the spindle of a spinning wheel.

Thankfully, I was yet to grant the child a gift. The fairy was very powerful and I could not counter her curse entirely, but I was certain I could soften its effects. 'You will prick your finger on a spindle in your eighteenth year, and you will fall asleep for a thousand more; you may be woken sooner by a loving word, else you will be safe behind the castle doors.'

'I've always wondered what a spinning wheel is,' Coral interrupted. 'I usually replace it with a sea urchin when I tell Chelle this story.'

'The surface-dwellers use spinning wheels to create thread from fibre,' the Sea Witch said.

'Thread? Fibre?'

'These concepts matter little. What matters is that every spinning wheel in the kingdom was burned at the order of the queen, with hope that the young princess might never prick her finger upon such a spindle.'

By her eighteenth year, the princess—who had been christened Hazel—had grown tired of staring at the same walls each day, and began exploring the kingdom and herself without telling her mother and father. She would dress in servants' clothes and flirt with the boys and girls her age, each of whom was fascinated by her. They would give Princess Hazel gifts of pressed flowers and tentative kisses.

While in town and unknown, the princess spoke to the townsfolk—to the bakers and the butchers—and because they were unaware of her stature, they discussed their thoughts openly. It brought Princess Hazel great wisdom and insight, which would have made her a fine ruler.

One day, she visited the tailor. The tailor owned the only spinning wheel that had not been burned after the proclamation of the old fairy. He had been instructed to lock it away and use it only to make the thread he needed to keep the kingdom clothed. He understood the importance of such a rule, but he didn't see the harm in teaching a simple servant girl how to use the rare contraption.

Princess Hazel sat before the spinning wheel, hoisting her skirts as the tailor guided her foot towards the pedal. The tailor pointed to the spindle and Princess Hazel reached for the slender rod, before a singular rose of blood bloomed from her index finger. She fell to the tailor's floor.

But, thankfully, my spell worked and Princess Hazel did not die. Rather, she fell into a deathly sleep. Once her disappearance was discovered and her lifeless body found, she was hidden in her bedroom. She was propped upon twenty cushions, the locked door protected by the head of the royal guard.

I was led from my home to the castle, where the queen met with me in the throne room, grey clouds gathering against the windows. 'What is the loving word that I must speak to wake my daughter?' she asked.

'I am sorry, your majesty, but I do not know.'

'You cast this spell, and yet you do not know the meaning of it?'

'I know its meaning well, but I cannot tell you the word that must be uttered or who must say it; that is dependent on the word Princess Hazel most wants to hear and who she most needs to hear it from.'

Though there was nothing more I could offer, the queen was unsatisfied with my answer and instructed me to stay in the castle while she sat by Princess Hazel's bedside and whispered every word that she could think of, her cadence overflowing with a mother's love. When the princess did not wake, the king tried, listing strings of syllables, each stitched together with a father's care. Princess Hazel's extended family, the royal guard, and even the servants tried, but the princess did not awaken.

When those residing within the castle failed to wake their daughter, the queen and king extended the invitation across the land. Princess Hazel's family learnt of their daughter's adventures as many of those she had spoken with or shared affection with arrived, their hearts filled with hope. Each was unsuccessful, but Princess Hazel's consciousness lived on in the stories these guests shared with the queen and king over dinner, teaching them of her generosity and love.

Princess Hazel's slumber outlasted the lives of the queen, the king, and the royal guard, but I remained in the castle and encouraged thorny vines to cover the castle doors and grow around her tower, protecting her as her parents had always sought to. As the story of the old fairy's curse faded, another royal family from another palace claimed the land.

People wondered at what could be hiding within the abandoned castle of the forgotten princess. In the decades that I had lived with Princess Hazel, I had not remained unnoticed, and rumours spread. Brave adventurers began to travel across the land with plans to climb the spire and slay the evil troll.

Many tried and most failed to reach the princess, unable to pass the shield of brambles that my magic had wrapped around the stone, but one man—a prince from several kingdoms away—managed to climb the tower by wrapping his hands in strips of leather. He entered the castle through Princess Hazel's window and saw me, sitting at her bedside.

The prince raised his sword and thrust it towards me, but when he saw Princess Hazel's curled hair strewn across the twenty cushions upon which she rested, he hesitated. 'Did you kill this beautiful princess?' he asked.

'I saved her from death,' I replied. 'She is only sleeping.'

The prince walked to her bedside and shook Princess Hazel gently by the arm, then more roughly by the shoulder. 'If she is sleeping, why does she not wake?'

'It is a magic slumber, designed to protect her from a horrible curse.'

The prince sheathed his sword. 'I came here to conquer this castle and the troll that lives within it,' he said, 'but now I must succeed in waking this princess. Tell me, what must I do?'

'She will wake only after one thousand years of rest unless she hears a loving word from a particular person, though I know not what nor who.'

'What's her name?' the prince asked.

'Hazel,' I replied.

'Hazel,' he mused, and the princess woke.

❦

'And they lived happily ever after,' Coral concluded.

'Don't get ahead of yourself,' the Sea Witch said. 'You weren't there and you don't know what happened next. Let me tell you.'

❦

Though conscious, Princess Hazel struggled to keep her eyes open, and when she did manage, those glassy orbs stared past the prince and me, finding shapes on the ceiling.

'I only had to speak her name?' asked the prince.

'A name can be awfully powerful, particularly when spoken with conviction and care,' I replied.

'If such a thing is true, then I should tell you that my name is Prince Alder. What should I call the wise woman who protected Princess Hazel through her deathly sleep?'

'I once lived beneath a bridge in a forest far away and there I lost my need for a name, so I tossed it into the river; I am yet to find a new one,' I replied.

I brought Princess Hazel fresh water from the well and a meal made from the root vegetables that I spent years tending in the castle gardens.

When she was well enough to consume them, I sat on the bed and held a glass to her lips. 'Slowly,' I encouraged as she threatened to drown herself by drinking the entire jug of water in as few mouthfuls as possible.

'What happened?' Princess Hazel asked as soon as she found her voice.

I told her and Prince Alder the tale of the curse at the christening and my attempt to save her, and the princess recalled the rare spinning wheel that the tailor sought to show her. I had not known that Princess Hazel had been sneaking into the town, disguised as a servant, until she revealed it over the stew we all shared that night.

'The prince spoke the word that you needed to hear with the voice and intonation that your soul was waiting for, and you woke from your cursed slumber.'

'Why did my parents not just tell me about the curse?' she asked. 'If I had known, I would not have gone near the tailor's workshop.'

'I believe they did not want to scare you, and with no spinning wheels in the castle, they assumed that you would be safe.'

'Where are they?' Princess Hazel asked. 'I want to apologise for leaving the castle when they were only trying to protect me by asking me to stay within these walls.'

'Prince Alder woke you before you reached the thousandth year of your slumber, but you have still been asleep for a very long time. Approximately three centuries,' I said.

'And my parents?'

'They lived long, fulfilling lives and died

peaceful, natural deaths,' I replied.

Princess Hazel cried for her mother and father, for her extended family, the royal guard, the servants, the abandoned castle, and the lost kingdom. Prince Alder tried to hold her close, but she refused him. 'Why did it have to be you who broke the curse?' she asked. 'Why did it have to take so long for me to wake?'

I left Princess Hazel to her sadness so that I might seek leaves that could be brewed into a soothing tea. When I bought the pot and cups back to the bedroom, Princess Hazel had fallen asleep on Prince Alder's chest.

The following day, Prince Alder returned to his horse and rode back towards his kingdom, to inform his own family that he had not perished at the hands of an evil troll. He promised to return.

In his absence, I took Princess Hazel on short walks through the forest to help her regain her strength, and fed her stews and soups. Her cheeks, pale and hollow, found a glow that reminded me of sunrise. We talked about the time before she fell asleep, where she was carefree in her travels of the kingdom, the ruins of which surrounded us.

'I could go anywhere if I wore the right outfit,' she said. 'The ball gowns I was made to wear never suited me, and they scared the townsfolk, but if I approached them in dull tones and torn fabrics, they treated me as though I was one of their own. I was courted by women as often as men, and I was happy sharing my love with anyone if their jokes made me laugh. I'm not sure what that made me, but it certainly made me different, and that just fascinated people more. I guess that's all gone now.'

'Your kingdom isn't all there was; there are many other kingdoms and many other people, if you wish to leave the castle you've always known. There are many labels across the kingdoms for those who are different like us—some used by others, and some we choose ourselves—but not every kingdom is as welcoming of those who love freely as yours once was.'

'Then perhaps it's better if I don't know them.'

❧

'What do you mean when you say "different"?' Coral asked.

'Princess Hazel was always attracted to both men and women, and perhaps those who dance between the genders; I too am attracted to whomever brings me joy, regardless of how they identify.'

'And on the surface there are labels for such a thing?'

'Are there not here?'

'Not that I know,' Coral said. 'I've never even met somebody who feels such a way.' 'Except you do,' the Sea Witch said.

'How did you...'

The Sea Witch laughed. 'I always know,' she said. 'There are more terms than those that I know, and more people still who prefer not to use them at all, but it can be nice to feel as though you belong. It was a long time ago that I heard the word "queer", and it's the word I use for myself if asked. There was a girl I met in a forest once who proudly called herself "pansexual". In a distant market I found the term "bisexual", I have encountered a prince who used the label "omnisexual", and once I met a water spirit who referred to herself simply as "fluid".'

Coral flicked her tail, sending currents of water through the cave. 'I like fluid,' she said. 'I wonder if I'm that.'

'Perhaps,' the Sea Witch replied. 'But nobody can tell you who you are.'

The word inhabited Coral's mouth like a bubble, filling her with fragile buoyancy. 'What happened to Princess Hazel?' she asked, seeking distraction.

When Prince Alder returned, he helped Princess Hazel to continue her regular walks while I used my magic to gently pry the thorny vines from the castle's exterior and polish the discoloured stone beneath, helping the princess to reclaim the castle she did not wish to leave. I refurbished the paintings, polished the mirrors, and put vases of fresh flowers on every surface.

'The castle is starting to look like a home again,' Princess Hazel said as we all gathered around the dining table one evening. 'Thank you.'

Prince Alder walked with Princess Hazel through the forests and around the ruins each morning, unless he was away from the castle visiting his family. He did this often, always with the promise that he would return. Princess Hazel regained her strength in what felt like the shortest time, though I had been wandering the halls of this castle alone for so long that I had little understanding of what time was anymore; saplings in the forest seemed to grow into trees overnight.

One evening when Prince Alder returned to the castle, he sought me in my chambers. 'May I speak with you?' he asked.

'Of course.'

'I wish to ask Hazel to marry me and, as the woman who has rested by her bedside for so long, I sought to ask for your blessing.'

'How long has it been since you first arrived here?' I asked.

'It has just passed two years since I woke Hazel with her name, and in these months I have learnt much of her character. She has a remarkable understanding of a world that no longer exists and revels in the stories I share of the one she is yet to experience. She has plans for the kingdom on which this castle stands and I want to help her bring them to fruition. I hope that she feels the same for me as I do for her.'

'I would not wish to stand in the way of something that might bring Princess Hazel joy,' I said, 'but the decision is ultimately hers.'

The princess was hesitant, uncertain of what marriage signified in this new world. When assured that Prince Alder had no desire to return to his own kingdom with her as his prize, but rather wished for them to stay in her own castle, even though it meant relinquishing his own title, she accepted the carved wooden ring that he offered as a symbol of their union.

❦

'And *then* they lived happily ever after,' Coral insisted.

'It is easy to claim that a story ends when everything seems perfect, but the characters must always continue to live out their tale. Nothing is perfect forever,' the Sea Witch said.

❦

The princess and the prince, each without a kingdom to rule, simply became Hazel and Alder. They continued to take walks each morning, using the time to discuss their plans for the castle and the forgotten kingdom, revealing their dreams to me over dinners shared.

With a touch of magic, I helped Hazel to create a larger garden, which she tended each day while Alder carved figures from the branches he gathered in the forest. Soon their morning walks led them into nearby towns, where they sold their produce and carvings at markets I once frequented.

The pair began to build a stable for Alder's horse. I offered to help, but they wanted to feel the weight of the stone in their hands. They always came to dinner after dark and covered in mud, but with smiles as wide as the river where I once lived.

One night, over bowls of casserole and plates of freshly baked bread, Hazel asked, 'Alder, why don't you return home to see your family since you placed your ring upon my finger?'

'When I told my family of my choice to marry you and live with you here in your castle, they insisted that I stay with you always to protect you,' Alder replied.

'The wise woman always protected me, and now that I am awake I can protect myself,' Hazel said.

'I made a vow,' Alder explained, 'and I must honour it.'

'Well, if you must stay by my side, perhaps I could come with you to the old kingdom and meet your family.'

'I would rather you do not meet my family, and I would also rather not talk about it again,' Alder replied.

This was not the only fight Hazel and Alder ever had. Sometimes they bickered over less serious things, like the colour of the wallpaper they should use in the drawing room, and sometimes they disagreed over more serious topics, like whether they should have children. Although the arguments varied, they regularly returned to Hazel's unhappiness about having never met Alder's family, and his assurance that she never would.

'Can you at least tell me why not?' Hazel asked one night.

'Telling you why you cannot meet them would be as bad as taking you there,' Alder replied.

'What are you afraid of?'

'I am afraid of losing you.'

'And you think your family would stand between us?'

'I think you would not want to be with me

anymore if you knew about my family.'

'There is no truth about your family that would make me leave you,' Hazel said.

'And yet if that proves untrue, there is nothing I can do to return the words to my lips.'

'Have faith in me,' Hazel replied. 'You may have vowed to protect me, but I have also vowed to protect you. I will not go back on my word and I will not leave you over a truth that changes nothing.'

Alder considered this and, trusting Hazel, said, 'Well then, let me tell you a story.

There was once a great war in the mountain caves where the ogres had dwelt for centuries. Many of the ogres fled the conflict, and one found a manor in which to live and made a home for himself within its walls. Among the possessions the ogre brought with him were the many minerals and gemstones that he had found while mining in the mountain caves, and though they meant little to him, he used them to pay the people in his new land so that they would tend to the fields and share their bounty with him.

Many of the people who worked for the ogre were scared of him, though most had never spoken to him. One day a woman decided to go to the manor and seek an audience with the ogre to see if he truly was as frightful as the stories declared. Though she could understand little of what the ogre said, she recognised that he was not going to hurt her.

For a modest wage, she stayed with the

ogre and cooked for him, cleaned the manor's many rooms, and taught him enough of the local language for him to communicate with the others who worked for him. Though most remained scared of him, simply because of the bedtime fables they were told of bloodthirsty ogres, he appreciated her attempts and enjoyed learning new things.

Though many would not have believed it possible, the ogre and the woman had a child. The child appeared mostly human, but she grew taller than any man and lived twice as long. She worked as a blacksmith and was capable of carrying burdens the other workers could only dream of lifting.

'My mother was descended from this half-ogress,' Alder concluded, 'and thus, so was I.'

'I understand why you are fearful, but all I hear is the story of an ogre who sought knowledge and a woman who showed nothing but compassion, and I am proud to be married to a distant descendent of the half-ogress that their love brought into the world,' Hazel said.

'I am flawed,' Alder replied, 'and you deserve a story where you ride into the sunset with a perfect prince, not an imperfect man who gave up his title.'

'I do not wish to ride into any sunset, for I like it here; I do not need a kingdom to rule, for this castle is more than enough work; and I do not need your idea of a "perfect prince", for you are perfect for me.'

Soon after Alder told Hazel of his family, Hazel fell pregnant with their first child. With the money they made selling produce and carvings, the pair hired someone to cook and someone to clean; they considered paying a gardener too, but even with her swollen belly, Hazel did not wish to give up the time she spent sitting in the dirt and soaking in the sun.

With my tasks of cooking and cleaning taken from me, I had time to explore the land near the castle during the long summer days. I found a place where the dirt of the forest became mixed with sand, and a narrow path led out to the shore. I had never seen a beach before—only a riverbank—and the swell of the waves fascinated me. They distorted my face as I peered into the water and created a version of my features that I wanted to assume.

I spent most of my days with my bare feet in the water and I wondered what lay beneath the expanse of shallow turquoise and deep navy; after the birth of Hazel and Alder's daughter—whom they named Viridis—I decided that I should find out. I did not wish to spend another lifetime alongside a family that was not my own.

I joined Hazel and Alder for their walk one morning, as Hazel cradled Viridis and pointed to the trees.

'I have been meaning to tell you something,' I said. 'I have spent several centuries in this land, and many of them in this castle, and I think it is time for me to move on.'

'Move on?' Hazel asked.

'The castle only became my home when you

became my responsibility, but it wasn't always so; now that you have started to fill its halls with your own family again, it is time for me to find a new place to explore.'

I do not know what became of Hazel and Alder. Perhaps they are still together, bickering over wallpaper and raising their daughter, or perhaps time has changed their lives as it does the tide. All I know is that they were happy enough when I left them there—a forgotten princess, a part-ogre prince, and their kingdom-less castle—but that's not quite a happily ever after.

❦

Since the Sea Witch commenced her tale, Coral's eyes had adjusted to the faint glow emanating from her namesakes that clustered by the edges of the sea cave. In their luminescence she could determine the Sea Witch's features; her eyes were hooded with melancholy, memories of a distant place and time clouding her present.

'I hope Hazel and Alder are still happy together,' Coral said.

'I hope they are happy, wherever they are,' the Sea Witch replied.

'I think "happy enough" sounds nice, but do I still need a prince, a castle, and legs to be "happy enough" at the end of my story?'

'Just because a prince saved this princess, that doesn't mean a prince will also save the next. Anybody—regardless of gender, title, or tail—might have been the one who spoke Hazel's name with exactly the cadence she needed to hear. This same story may have taken place in a forest cabin or a beachside shack, a city skyscraper or an underwater cave. You tell stories to Chelle where you replace spindles with sea urchins; why not also switch princes for princesses, or legs for tails?'

'Chelle...' Coral said. 'If I don't need a prince, a castle, or a pair of legs for a happy ending, then maybe Chelle doesn't either.'

'That is sound logic,' the Sea Witch said.

'I have to go; I need to tell her.' Coral swam to the entrance of the cave, the dull light of the canyon just beyond reach. Before she turned to seek the brighter ocean, she paused. 'Sea Witch?'

'Yes?'

'Did you ever find yourself a new name?' 'I'm still looking,' the Sea Witch replied.

'Well, good luck,' Coral said, before her grey tail thrust her upwards and into the city.

'You're early,' Chelle said when Coral arrived. 'Did something happen?'

'I'm fine,' Coral replied. 'I didn't go to the surface today; I went to visit the Sea Witch.'

'You what? Going to the surface as often as you do is dangerous enough; you know that you shouldn't go anywhere near that canyon.'

'You're starting to sound like my father.'

'I'm sorry—you know I just care about you. I don't want to lose you, Coral, and I don't understand. Why did you go to see her?'

'I wanted to ask if she was able to give me legs so that I could live on the surface and find a castle and a prince. I thought maybe she could do the same for you and we could finally have our happily ever afters.'

'And what did she say?'

'Well, she said it was possible, but she made me listen to a story before she would do anything, and now I think I've changed my mind.'

'You don't want a happily ever after anymore? It must have been an incredible story. Can you tell it to me?'

'I could, but I don't think it's the best story to tell anymore. Let me share another with you.'

Coral began the tale that she had told Chelle the previous day at dusk, about the queen and king who longed for a child.

...and when the princess pricked her finger on a sea urchin, she fell into a deathly sleep. The royal guard carried her through the ocean to the Sea Palace and rested her upon the sand, and her family hoped for a way to break the spell.

Princes from across the ocean were invited to the palace to see if they could wake the princess, but none were successful. Princesses were also invited, but the princess stayed asleep. Word of her slumber spilled into the city and a woman—as attractive as she was clever—thought she might know the secret to breaking the curse. The woman swam to the palace and spoke to the royal guard.

'Are you a princess?' one guard asked.

'No,' the woman replied.

'Are you a noblewoman or someone of stature?'

'I am simply an artisan who lives on the edge

of the city and who has an idea,' the woman replied. 'If you believe you have another way to save the princess, then by all means close the palace doors to me, but if the king would like his daughter to be given every chance, lead me to her chambers.'

The woman was led into the palace and shown the princess, where she lay curled on the ocean floor, her tail as pale as bleached coral. At first, the woman circled the princess, considering her delicate form, before she swooped down towards the sand and kissed the princess on her cold lips.

To the surprise of everyone in the room, the princess woke.

There was a great feast to celebrate the occasion, and the woman from the edge of the city held the princess's hand beneath the table while they shared dessert and stories.

The princess's father wanted her to immediately marry the woman who saved her, but the princess and the woman disregarded him, deciding to take their time and let things blossom naturally, like the colourful anemones in the palace gardens.

At first the princess stayed at the palace and the woman stayed at her home on the edge of the city, where the princess visited her regularly. Before long, the princess moved in with the woman, for the palace was too crowded with fathers and grandmothers and so many sisters, and the woman's home was perfectly cosy. The princess and the woman enjoyed each other's company, laughing through the nights and sleeping beside one another on the ocean floor. And they...

'...lived happily ever after,' Chelle said.
   '...were happy enough,' Coral concluded.

13
OLIVE

Sometimes I have dreams about the day my sister left. Tabby placed her signet ring on my bedside table, so that I might wear it and remember her, but she did not wake me; she disappeared before the rooster crowed, the palace still trapped within the silence of slumber.

Tabby had always told me everything, but she never revealed where she was going; I often wondered if she even knew the answer herself when she first left through the palace gates. My parents asked where their second daughter was, but when I told the truth, they did not believe me. My parents and I rarely spoke after that, and when we did, they would stare at the signet ring adorning my finger with a mix of bitterness and melancholy. My mother barely looked at me, even as she died.

One day, I looked into the darkness of the well and lost myself there, in memories of my sister, when the signet ring slipped from my finger and fell into the depths. I heard the whispered clinks of the metal bouncing on the bricks, and then silence.

Shock stifled my cry.

'Excuse me,' called an echoing voice. 'Did somebody up there drop a ring just now?'

'Yes, I did,' I shouted into the well.

'Why did you do that?' the voice asked.

'I didn't mean to,' I said. 'It fell. Who are you?'

'My name is Hyla,' the voice replied. 'Who are you?'

'I am Princess Olive, daughter of King Twain. Would you kindly bring my ring back to me?'

'I will,' Hyla replied. 'But on one condition.'

'What condition?'

'That you do a simple favour for me.'

'Before I agree to anything, I want proof that you can return my ring to me,' I replied. I was met with no response.

I waited by the edge of the well for some time, catching my silent tears before they reached my chin, but I slowly grew certain that whomever I had heard in the depths of the well was not coming to meet me. In fact, I began to wonder whether there had truly been a voice at all.

I returned to the palace, passed the guards who were gathered in the palace gardens, and returned to my chambers where my tears ceased to be silent. The sound of my cries eventually reached my father, who came and stood by the door.

'What's wrong, Olive?'

'I lost Tabby's signet ring; it slipped into the well.'

My father approached the bed and placed a heavy hand on my shaking shoulder. 'Don't worry,' he said. 'We'll get it back, somehow.'

A cough by the bedroom door startled us. 'I am sorry for interrupting, your majesty and your highness,' said the leader of the royal guard, 'but somebody is waiting for you on the palace steps, Princess Olive. They say that their name is Hyla and that they have your sister's signet ring. They would not allow us to return it to you; they mentioned you had offered a reward for its return and they wanted to give the ring back to you directly.'

I leapt from the bed and rushed down the halls, out to the palace gardens where a person was waiting, admiring the flowers. 'You must be Hyla.'

'Your highness,' Hyla replied. 'I apologise for the time it takes to travel the tunnels adjoining the well shaft; though I journey them often, they are still long and winding. When I reached the well's edge, you were gone.'

'I wasn't sure you would ever come,' I replied.

'I understand. I also apologise for not giving your sister's signet ring back to the royal guard when they demanded it, but I wanted to discuss my small request with you further.'

'What is the favour you seek?'

'I would like to spend a day with you,' Hyla said. 'I would like to walk with you across the kingdom, talk with you about your life, share meals with you at your dining table, and sleep in your bedroom alongside you.'

'And whyever would you want that?'

Hyla hesitated, many words dancing behind their eyes.

I considered myself to be an excellent judge of character, but I was unable to understand Hyla. Everything about them was indeterminate: their hair was so streaked with dirt that its colour was hidden, their lips held a slight smile but their emotions were unknown, and their gender was confused by contrasts that my mind couldn't categorise. Hyla had torn pants but pointed features, short hair but a high voice, a flat chest but a narrow waist, and I struggled to find a pattern.

Perhaps this uncertainty was what bothered me most. Women who wished to spend time with me likely idolised me and sought to befriend me, while most men who asked to walk with me were seeking my hand in marriage or a night in my chambers. Hyla had asked to sleep alongside me, but not with me, and I knew not what that meant.

Regardless of Hyla's intentions, I knew that my father would not approve of my spending a day in their company, let alone the ongoing companionship that they may desire.

'I think perhaps I am different to anyone you have ever spent time with and that a day in my company would change the way you see the world,' Hyla finally replied.

'And what makes you think I want to see the world differently?' I replied. 'Stop holding my sister's ring for ransom and return my property to me immediately.'

'Sure,' Hyla replied, passing me the golden band. 'I don't want to manipulate you so that you must spend time with me; it must be a decision freely made. All I ask is that you remember my request— my offer—and if you ever wish to spend a day with me, simply return to the well any day before noon and call my name.'

I returned to my chambers, where my father waited. 'Did this Hyla person truly have Tabby's ring?' he asked when he saw me in the doorway.

I extended my hand, the band shining on my finger.

'And what was the reward they requested?' my father prompted.

'Hyla wishes to spend a day with me.'

'No desire for gold or jewels? They only want to spend a day in the company of my beautiful daughter? And truly, who wouldn't? I assume you agreed with their terms?'

'I do not know anything about this person. I do not understand their intentions and I do not feel comfortable inviting them into our home,' I said.

'You'd best be joking,' my father said. 'You must go back and allow Hyla to spend a day with you, and hope that they have not spread word of your refusal too far. I do not want a dissatisfied kingdom.'

I did not know where to find Hyla that afternoon, so I returned to the well the following morning, unable to deny the request of my father. I called into the darkness, 'Hyla, are you there?'

'Princess Olive?' came the reply.

'Yes. I have come to accept your offer of spending the day with you.' 'Wait where you are—I'll be there as quickly as I can.'

While I waited, I tossed pebbles into the well, listening to them clunk and clatter off the stone. Some of the pebbles called back to me for what seemed like forever, and the soft sound of water marked the end of their journeys, while others seemed to find their destination too early, suddenly and soundlessly, as they disappeared into the openings of caves and passageways. I stared into the darkness long enough that I became convinced I could see the water's surface, and with it my reflection.

'So, when I return to the tunnels and find a pile of rocks waiting for me, I know who to blame,' Hyla said.

'Sorry,' I replied, suddenly flustered. I stood, trying to regain my composure, and the collection of pebbles I had gathered in my lap clattered to the ground.

'It's fine,' Hyla said, laughing, 'and if you would like to continue throwing pebbles into the well, I will happily sit and join you.'

'I assure you, I don't normally do things like this; I was simply waiting for you.'

'Well what does a princess like you usually do with a morning as fine as this one?'

'I'm not sure,' I replied. 'I came to find you before I had breakfast, so perhaps I should return to the palace so that my servants can prepare me something. You may join me.'

We sat across from one another at the dining table and I tried to avoid looking directly at Hyla; I found the storm clouds brewing in their eyes distracting and—possibly—attractive, and the thought unsettled me. The servants, uncertain of what Hyla would like to eat, positioned an assortment of delicious breakfast foods between us.

'Do you always eat so lavishly?' Hyla asked.

'Some days.'

'Do you ever think of those who do not have enough to eat?'

I wondered at the question. 'Of course there are some with less than us, but are there truly some with so little that they cannot eat?' I asked.

My father entered the dining hall before Hyla could respond. His eyes darted between each side of the table, assessing us. 'Who's this?' he asked.

'This is Hyla. Remember, you told me to invite Hyla to spend a day with me as a reward for returning Tabby's signet ring?'

'You didn't tell me that Hyla was...' my father trailed off.

'I tried to imply...' I started.

'I thought you simply did not wish to reveal your hero's gender because you were embarrassed that a young man was interested in you; I never considered that it was because they were one of... *them*.' He turned his attention to Hyla. 'Leave,' he commanded, his eyes shimmering with cold glass.

I watched on silently as Hyla abandoned their half-finished plate of breakfast and left the palace.

'I'm sorry, Olive. I should have trusted your judgement when you said you did not feel comfortable bringing this Hyla character into our home,' my father said.

'Maybe,' I replied, pushing back my chair. I strode from the dining hall, leaving my father standing alone and uncomfortable in the centre of the expansive, yet suddenly suffocating space.

When I found the sun, Hyla was already far ahead on the path; I removed my shoes so that I could jog to catch up with them. 'Hyla,' I called.

Hyla seemed more surprised to see me following them along the path than they had when they were sent from the palace grounds. 'What are you doing?' they asked.

'I promised I would spend the day with you, so here I am.'

'Your father said that he *made* you fulfil my wishes; I do not want to spend time with you if it is not of your choosing.'

'You're right,' I said. 'I didn't choose to return to the well this morning, but I chose to follow you now. I disagree with what my father did in the breakfast hall; he treated you as though you aren't truly a person, and I don't think I want to be like that.'

'Well, since we have been banished from the palace, what would you like to do?' Hyla asked.

'I rarely leave the palace grounds; since Tabby left and my mother died, my father doesn't let me stray far. What is there to do?'

'Come with me,' Hyla replied.

The kingdom was built against the side of a mountain that I had spent many years looking up at, but never neared. Hyla led me to the base of the towering landmass. Here, a narrow path was cut into the rock, winding up between the trees.

Hyla climbed fearlessly while the stones cut into my bare feet; I refused to speak of my discomfort. Before long we reached a section of stone that jutted out over the steep decline, and I followed Hyla out onto its smooth surface.

From the stone, I could see the kingdom. The palace was at one edge, surrounded by lush gardens and bright colours. The path from the palace stairs led through a white and gold town, and I could determine the grey stone of the well. I traced the path as the colours faded and became darker, like a flowerbed that had been splattered with mud. Some parts of the kingdom were in shadow so black that they looked like a forest after a brushfire ripped through, like the one I once compared my sister to.

'Why does so much of the kingdom look like that?' I asked.

'You truly don't know?'

'Know what?'

'At the very least, I'm sure you are aware of the strict rules King Twain has against anything that might be deemed... different?' Hyla asked.

'When my mother became ill, she claimed it was because everything was changing around her; my father tried to help her by hiding anything she did not understand.'

'That meant hiding people like me,' Hyla said. 'He built a wall through the kingdom and we were sent to live behind it so that we did not tarnish the purity of the palace's surrounds. Beyond the wall live the genderless and the genderfluid, the gays and lesbians and queer There too live our families, should they support us enough to stay with us where there is little food and less wealth. Anyone who dares to break the rules that keep the gender binary intact is deemed to be too different for the town near the palace; I once saw a man carried beyond the wall for crying when his mother died.'

'Men aren't supposed to cry,' I said. 'Says who?'

'My father.'

'Well, maybe he's wrong,' Hyla replied.

A heavy silence descended, but Hyla quickly interrupted it. 'We never did finish breakfast—let's get something to eat.'

I met Hyla's parents at the little house that they shared with another family. 'We didn't know we would be cooking lunch for company,' Hyla's mother said when they arrived.

'And royal company, no less,' Hyla's father said. 'Hyla is always forgetting to share important news with us.'

'Hyla didn't know I would be joining you for lunch,' I said. 'In fact, I didn't know I would be until a short while ago. Please, don't overexert yourselves for my sake.'

But Hyla's mother and father gathered all of their food to ensure there was enough for everyone. I knew that Hyla's family had little to spare and I felt immense guilt as I raised my fork to my mouth, but I also did not want to seem unappreciative. 'This is lovely,' I said.

'Thank you,' Hyla's mother replied. 'I am so pleased you think so.'

After lunch, Hyla took me on a short tour of their house. The space was too cramped for them and their parents, let alone the other family who shared their kitchen and dining area, and the single bathroom. Tiles had fallen from the walls to expose the plaster and glue, and in places the plaster had also peeled away, revealing joists and insulation.

'How do you live here?' I asked Hyla.

'We don't have a choice, so we manage. There's a reason I spend most of my time in the tunnels adjoining the well, or climbing the mountain overlooking the kingdom.'

Angry, I suddenly cared little for the opinions of my father. 'We must return to the palace,' I said.

As we passed the wall and entered the pristine streets lined with spacious houses, Hyla tensed. I took their hand, lacing my fingers with theirs, comforting them. I led Hyla up the palace stairs, the cold stone comforting my bare, blistered feet.

I disregarded the disapproving stares of the palace guards as I passed them and entered the wide hallway. The luxury once brought me joy, but now the expansive space served only as a symbol of waste; I owned so much and used so little, while there were people in our kingdom who were cramped and hungry. Made timid by the palace walls, Hyla's hand escaped my grasp, but they still followed as I marched into the throne room where my father was seated on a pedestal of red and gold.

'Father.'

'What are you doing back in my palace?' he asked, addressing Hyla.

'Hyla is my guest and I am speaking to you,' I responded.

'I am not speaking to you while you are speaking like that.' 'Are you aware of the poverty our kingdom is facing?'

'It is not our kingdom—it is *my* kingdom—and my subjects are not impoverished.'

'They do not have food to eat, space to live in, or freedom to be themselves. Families are sharing their homes with one another because they cannot afford to live in houses of their own. People are afraid, and those who live differently have been forced into hiding.'

'Those who are different are hidden from the rest of us for good reason,' my father said.

'What, to save my mother? Mother was distraught

because her life suddenly changed—she lost one daughter to the night and pushed the other away—but her aversion to these differences does not mean all things that are different from her, or us, needed to be hidden from the light. It didn't help her, did it?'

'My subjects are happy.'

'Your subjects are starving.'

'Those beyond the wall are not my subjects.'

'They are ruled by you and they struggle at your hand. They are people, and they deserve to be treated as such.'

'Those who refuse to live law-abiding lives—who wish to flaunt their uniqueness, who choose not to embody the gender they were given at birth, who do not fulfil the roles they are destined to perform, and who wish to live in alternative ways and with people who are the same gender as themselves—are not truly people.'

'So your daughter—Tabby—is not truly a person?'

'What do you mean?'

'Tabby always loved women as much as she loved men; surely you spent enough time with her to notice that.'

'You have a fascinating imagination, Olive. We both know Tabby was not of that kind.'

'Well then, maybe you are saying that I am not a person.'

'Now what are you on about?'

'You have brought many princes to the palace to meet with me, and while they have all been attractive and some have been kind, none have been appropriate suitors. I have only spent one day with Hyla, and I think I want to spend another. Maybe many more. Perhaps that means you think I should live without food or space or freedom.'

My father considered this for a moment, his eyes searching the room. 'I certainly do not think you should starve, Olive, or that you should live without space to thrive. Regardless of how you live, you are my daughter, and I love you. Perhaps it is unfair of me to prioritise the wellbeing of my daughter before the subjects of my kingdom, but you must understand that these are people I have never met and have rarely seen.'

'Maybe that should change, father,' I said.

'I think you're right.'

I reached out to Hyla and squeezed their hand.

'As for Hyla,' my father said, 'I do not approve of you committing yourself to anyone from the town, let alone somebody whose gender is an utter mystery. You are a princess and your eventual marriage is greater than you; it should strengthen our kingdom, expand our reaches, and act as a symbol of joy for our people.'

'Nobody's talking about marriage just yet,' I said, but he held a hand out to silence me.

'I spoke similarly of the importance of marriage to Tabby once, and I never saw her again. I've never seen you happy before and I do not wish to stand between you and happiness; I will not lose the only family that I have left. Just... take it slow, would you Olive? The kingdom has been this way for so long that I have forgotten what change looks like.'

'We'll figure it out together,' I said.

When I woke the following morning, I was sprawled across the rug on the floor of my chambers, still dressed in my clothes from the day before. Hyla was there, curled up nearby.

We had shared stories into the evening until our last moments of consciousness so that, accidentally, Hyla's last request—to sleep alongside me—had been fulfilled.

Hyla's short, curled hair covered their face, each steady breath moving the strands. I reached over and tucked them safely behind their ear. I wondered if I should wake them so that we might find another mountain path to climb or underground tunnel to explore, but they looked so peaceful in their slumber; I let them rest.

14
IVORY

Ivory and Jett sat by the ashes of the fire that their parents had built, listening for shuffling sounds in the forest. 'They aren't coming back, sis,' Jett said.

'They're our mother and father; they have to come back,' Ivory replied.

'I overheard them talking last night. They said that if they didn't leave us in the forest, then we were all going to starve.'

'Then what do you propose we do?'

Jett stood and walked to the edge of the clearing, pointing at the white pebbles shining in the dusk light. 'I left a trail behind us just in case we were left here, so now we can return to the village on our own. Are you coming with me?'

'What's the point of going back if they don't want us in the village?'

'Where else is there to go?'

'Who knows?' Ivory stood and walked away from the trail, leaving the clearing and striding into the trees.

Jett followed. 'I don't know about this, sis.'

'Surely our village isn't the only one around here. There must be somewhere else where people don't know us, and perhaps they aren't stricken by the drought,' Ivory said.

'But if they don't know us, who's to say they will feed us, even if their crops continue to grow?'

'We're young; perhaps they will feel sorry for us?'

'I'm thirsty,' Jett said.

Ivory and Jett walked for an hour and a half, which to them felt like an eternity. They stumbled upon a river, and Jett rushed towards it, but when he raised a palm of water to his lips, all he tasted was salt. He spat and spluttered, and was thirstier than before.

Ivory knelt beside Jett and brought the water to her face, washing the sweat and tears from her cheeks, and dirt from her hands. When the pair looked at their twisted reflections side-by-side in the shifting water, they were reminded of how similar they seemed, and yet how different they were.

The twins had the same long, dark curls around their faces, yet Jett's made him look handsome while Ivory's seemed unkempt. Both had always been loud and opinionated, yet Jett's opinions made him strong—a leader—while Ivory's made her seem bossy. The pair had been caught sitting on the steps of the school once, commenting on which of the girls were the prettiest as they walked by, and while Jett was patted on the back for such chatter, Ivory was chastised.

'You are not to like the young girls the way your brother does,' their teacher said, peering out at them through the distorted glass of the schoolroom windows. 'You should be looking at the young boys, not the girls.'

'I look at the boys too though, ma'am,' Ivory replied.

'You don't know what you want,' the teacher said. 'You're only a child.'

Ivory had been made to sit in a classroom on her own for the rest of the midday break.

The twins saw the smoke first, and then they saw the rooftop. 'A cottage?' Jett asked. 'We must be getting close to a village.' But as they approached, they realised it was simply one cottage in the middle of the forest.

'Who lives out here on their own?' Ivory asked.

'I heard a story once about a woman who was sent into the forest because she was a witch. She used to live in our village until she cursed a girl in her class at school, and the village banded together to banish her. Maybe this is where the witch lives?'

'I didn't think you believed in magic,' Ivory said.

'I don't,' Jett replied.

'But you believe in a witch?'

'I don't know. I just think we need to be careful before we go–'

But Ivory had already opened the squeaky gate that led to the cottage garden and was crossing the stepping stones towards the door.

The cottage was made of wood and bark of different shapes, attached to each other roughly with nails that had rusted so that they looked like chocolate buttons. The timber was burnt in places, and it reminded Ivory of the gingerbread she had tried to make with her mother once, years ago, back when ginger and flour and sugar weren't so scarce. Ivory knocked on the door.

Something about the woman who answered made her seem older than Ivory and Jett's parents, yet she stood perfectly straight and her face was hardened. She seemed surprised to see a person on her doorstep and another trailing behind, navigating the stepping stones.

'What are you two children doing out in the forest by yourselves?' the woman asked.

'We are not children,' Jett declared.

'Hush, Jett,' Ivory said. 'Our parents took us into the forest and left us in a clearing while they went in search of firewood; they never came back. We think we were left behind because of the drought in the village—people are starving and our parents could not look after us anymore.'

'Your parents just left you out here?' the woman asked. 'Well, come in. I have plenty of food and water to share.'

The woman held the door open and Ivory walked past her, seeking a seat at the dining table. Jett hesitated, his thoughts lingering on the tale of the witch, certain that this woman was secretly planning to curse them like the girl in his class at school.

'Don't worry,' the woman said. 'You're safe here. And you must be so hungry and thirsty.'

Jett was very hungry and extremely thirsty, so he swallowed his fear and walked into the cottage so he could sit beside his sister.

The woman brought the children bowls of fruit and vegetables, as well as glasses of water and juice. Jett sniffed each item suspiciously before raising it to his lips to gently nibble at its edges, while Ivory ate with little hesitation, guided by her weeks of hunger.

'What are you doing living out here in the forest, alone?' Ivory asked between mouthfuls.

'When I was young, I lived in the village, but I was banished to the forest when I was about your age. I built myself a shelter to keep out the rain at night and I searched the surrounds for somewhere else—another village, another person—but I found nothing. There is only the village and, now, this cottage that I call my home.'

'What did you do to be banished to the forest?' Jett asked.

'What did you do?' the woman countered. 'Sometimes we need not do anything wrong to be left behind by those who are supposed to care for us.'

'What's your name?' Ivory asked.

'Alene.'

Once the twins were hydrated and their stomachs full, Alene offered them a place to sleep on beds made from bundles of hand-sewn rugs and sheets. Ivory wrapped herself in the warmth she was offered and fell asleep quickly, while Jett stayed awake, certain the woman would return to the room in the middle of the night to hurt them with her wicked spells.

When the cottage was quiet and still, an owl called; Jett gasped and Ivory woke. 'Are you okay?' she whispered.

'Are you not the least bit scared?' Jett asked, his heartbeat deafening him.

'Of course I'm scared,' Ivory replied, 'but I can do little to protect us without a good night's rest and a decent meal. I know you are worried that Alene is a witch, and of course we should be cautious, but do you think she would be eating the same food as us if it were poisonous?'

Jett thought about this for a moment. 'I suppose not.'

'Be thoughtful, brother, and choose your battles.'

In the morning, Ivory woke before her brother and heard noise outside the cottage. She went to a window, scared that the sound was of wolves or bears—or perhaps something even worse. Peering out into the dawn, she saw only Alene, crouched in the garden; Ivory walked out to join her.

'You're up early,' Alene said.

'I slept well,' Ivory replied. 'Your garden is beautiful.'

'Most of the vegetables are grown from wild varieties I found in the forest.'

'Who taught you how to grow them?'

'I taught myself.'

The garden was lush, the damp soil covered in decomposing leaves taken from the forest floor. 'I have never seen this much food in one place,' Ivory said. 'This is amazing.'

'The village used to have a garden like this. Is it really all gone?'

'The sky still clouds over, but the rain hasn't reached the village in months.'

'Do you want to go back?'

'I don't have any friends, the teacher punishes me constantly, and my parents abandoned me in the forest; I'm not sure I have a place in the village.'

'I wish there was somewhere else I could take you, so that you would be safe,' Alene said. 'Although, I suppose, if you wanted... I could make space for you here. You could help me build a new room for you and your brother, and I could teach you how to grow crops.'

'I would have to talk to Jett about it.'

'Of course,' Alene said. 'But now, since you're here, could you help me for a moment?'

Alene pointed at a spot in the dirt and Ivory dug little trenches with a trowel while Alene planted potatoes.

When Alene and Ivory returned to the house, dirt beneath their fingernails, Jett was yawning and stretching exaggeratedly, trying to disguise his guilt for snooping while he had been alone.

'The next task on the list for today is to cut some more firewood,' Alene said. 'I would very much appreciate assistance from both of you.' Alene fetched her axe and Ivory went to follow her as she left for the forest, but Jett caught her arm.

'I watched you helping Alene through the cottage window,' Jett said, 'and I saw all of the food she grows here. We should steal her crops and take them back with us to the village.'

'We cannot steal Alene's crops.'

'Why not?' Jett replied. 'We could help everyone and our parents would be able to take us back. And anyway, Alene owes the village. Even if she isn't a witch, she still must have done something awful for them to banish her like this.'

'She doesn't owe the village; the village owes her. They left her out in the forest to die, just like our parents left us.'

'And our parents had good reason; they wouldn't have left us here if they had enough food to look after us. If we took Alene's crops...'

'We were not taught to steal,' Ivory said.

'But we were taught to protect our family.'

Tired of fighting with her stubborn brother, and knowing they would never agree, Ivory left to help Alene.

Even without his sister's support, Jett was certain he was right, so as Alene and Ivory's voices became muffled by the closed door, he stole a basket from Alene's kitchen and took it into the garden, where he began to load the woven wicker with crops.

When the basket was nearly full, Jett hesitated, uncertain of how much food he should leave behind.

'It's fine,' Alene said. 'You can fill it to the top.'

Startled, Jett dropped the basket and leapt to his feet. 'Please don't hurt me,' he said.

'I'm not going to hurt you,' Alene replied. 'Why are you afraid of me? If you wanted food to take back to the starving families in the village, you only needed to ask. If I'd known how badly they were affected by drought—and if I thought anyone in the village would have been happy to see my face—I would have brought food to them long ago.'

'You're not going to hurt me?'

'Of course not; I'm not a monster.'

'And you're not a witch?'

'A witch? Is that what you thought?'

'That's what they say in the village. They say that years ago a witch was banished to the forest because she cursed a girl with whom she shared a class at school, and that the witch still lives in the forest alone.'

'Well, I was banished and I do live in the forest, but I'm certainly not a witch.'

'I told you, brother,' Ivory said from the open window.

'But if you aren't a witch, what happened to the girl at school?' Jett asked.

Alene laughed. 'It feels so inconsequential now,' she said. 'We were caught kissing behind the school building.'

'That's all?' Ivory asked.

'But if you were both kissing, why were you the one taken into the forest?' Jett asked.

'I had always been a troublemaker and the girl I was kissing was the teacher's daughter, so the only explanation they believed was that I made her do it.'

'But you didn't, did you?' Ivory asked. 'The girl wanted to kiss you.'

'She did,' Alene said. 'Just like all the boys and girls who always kissed and giggled behind the sports shed, but none of them were banished to the forest when they were caught.'

'Our teacher told us that girls aren't allowed to like other girls.'

'My teacher told me that too,' Alene agreed.

'We're supposed to like boys instead,' Ivory said.

'You're supposed to do whatever makes you happy,' Alene said.

Jett had retrieved the fallen basket and held it before him. 'I'm sorry for taking your food.'

'Take it,' Alene said. 'Take it back to the village, to your family, and let them eat. I suppose you have a way of returning?'

'I used a trail of white pebbles to connect the village to the clearing where our family lit our campfire and made us stay. I used the same pebbles to connect the clearing to your cottage.'

'You are both welcome to follow your trail and return to the village whenever you wish. You are also welcome to stay here with me, or visit any time. It's entirely up to you.'

'Well of course we will be returning to the village—it's our home,' Jett said. 'We finally have a way of saving our friends and family, and we're going to take it, right Ivory?'

'I don't think I want to come with you, Jett. I am going to stay here with Alene. I don't fit in at the village and I don't want to be banished forever the next time the teacher overhears me talking about how pretty the other girls are. I want to stay here and learn all the skills that our teacher told us were only for boys, all the amazing things Alene can do.'

'I don't want to say goodbye to you, sis.'

'This isn't goodbye. I can always follow the trail of white pebbles to the village and visit you, and you can do the same to visit me.'

'And maybe one day the village can be your home again,' Jett said. 'A home for both you and Alene, and others like you.'

'Maybe,' Ivory said. 'But you will need to tell new stories of a woman that a village thought was a witch, but who was simply a girl who learnt to look after herself in the forest, and who is now teaching another to do the same.'

15
CLEMENCY

I met a girl who had lived a fraction of my life, who feared my presence and yet sought my wisdom. I told her stories that I had not considered for many years and, as she left my cave, I followed not long after. My face had not been touched by daylight for several lifetimes, but I was finally ready to seek the sun again.

I had returned to the darkroom several times since I began my journey, but never saw a sign of Innocence in the halls of our old house. No new photographs were hanging in the darkroom, but I always collected more of the old, discarded images to sell at markets and on streets. I cared little for the money, but I enjoyed the sense of purpose, before my time was taken up advising royal families and protecting sleeping princesses.

Even when I was convinced Innocence must have lived out her mortal life without returning to our shared home, I travelled back there from time to time, uncertain what I was looking for. I returned there again on the day I left the ocean, to find the fumes of developer barely masked by the scent of whiskey, the fragrant shadow of a life I had almost forgotten.

Sitting in her old armchair, rolls of film discarded on the floor, sat Innocence. Eternities had passed, too long for her mortal body to still be carrying her enchanted mind, yet I could only see the mark of the passing years in the colour of her aged eyes, as they looked up to meet mine.

'Where have you been?' she asked.

'To more worlds than I can count on these old hands,' I replied.

'How long has it been?'

'Forever.'

'And yet I feel as though I only just left,' she said.

'How are you still alive, Innocence?'

'It's funny to hear you speak that name. I've never heard it from your lips.'

'Is it still the name you call yourself?'

'Not that I deserve it.'

Innocence took a sip from the whiskey glass, still mostly full, and pursed her lips. 'It's not like I remember.'

'How does it taste?'

'Like captivity.'

Innocence rose, then stooped to gather the rolls of film piled by her feet like autumn leaves. I knelt to help her, and together we took armfuls of memories to the darkroom. Together, we brought into being the many worlds we had both seen, images of lives we lived without each other and within ourselves.

'I recognise this manor,' I said as swirling light and dark revealed familiar walls and roof. 'And this tower. This bridge. These forests.'

'You are not the only one who travelled far.'

'You never did say how you are still alive.'

'I was only gone for the stretch of winter; I returned from the city streets when the snow began to thaw.'

'And yet, in the space of a season, you visited all of the scenes that took me lifetimes to walk between?'

I walked through this world in my dreams, taking photographs of women who stood before me like mirrors, both of the person I am and the person I inhabited. I took photographs of these reflections and their homes, and whenever I woke, the rolls of film were waiting for me, as though I'd truly been there.'

'You have photographs of all the homes I grew restless in and of all the people I met, as though you were inside my mind and my eyes were your camera.'

'Can you tell me their stories?' Innocence asked.

So as we washed photographs and pinned them to the overhead lines, I told Innocence the stories of the women I had met, their partners, their friends, and the homes they inhabited. I told her of the struggles they faced, the journeys they conquered, and the ways I helped them find themselves. Centuries danced before us on shivering string.

'I wish I'd heard these stories long ago,' Innocence said, 'before the frost crept in and the Snow Queen called me to her mirror.'

'What good would that have done?'

'Tales of courage might have helped me find my own.'

Our life returned to a normal that I barely recalled, until it felt as though I'd never left home for all those years. Some days I dreamt of distant places still, but they became little more than stories, as the forest fruits fell and leaves began to change.

Innocence spent more time at her desk than she used to, pen in hand and whiskey glass stowed away. 'What are you working on?' I always asked, but she'd only shake her head.

One day, she approached, a stack of paper in her hand. 'It's finished.'

'What is?'

'The story of your travels. The places you went, the people you met. It's all here.'

'My travels?'

'I recorded the stories you told me that night in the darkroom; the ones I wish my mother could have shared at my bedside when I was a child.'

She lay the pages across my hands, surely too light to capture the eternity that I'd spent wandering. I wondered at the thought of these words finding their way back into worlds I had visited, to the children of children that I once met.

'There's only one thing missing,' Innocence said. 'With what name do I mark the cover?'

I traced my finger across the blank space where my moniker might belong. I could not recall the name that I had discarded. To my mind I had only been her love, and then, as I walked the worlds, I became the troll. Who was I now that so much had happened, and so much remained unchanged?

And then I realised. The answer had been simple, but it had taken me so long to see. I took the pen from Innocence and, in shaking letters, I signed the page.

AFTERWORD

When I was young, I was taught happiness was defined by whether the princess finds a prince to marry by the end of her tale. In fact, her tales weren't really hers at all—princesses were nameless, voiceless characters who fulfilled a role and taught a moral.

The fairy tales I read in my formative years left little room for grey areas and fluidity— genders were binary, gender roles were discrete, and sexuality was unexplored. As I matured and found more diverse stories, they still rarely engaged with the spaces between the binaries; I gradually learned that man–woman relationships were not the only option, but I was not exposed to the rainbow of alternatives until much later in life.

When you apply to study for a doctorate—as I did in 2015—you are expected to fill a gap in existing publications and research. In some fields, this might mean you need to find a rare species of prawn and study its breeding habits under specific conditions. For my creative writing degree, the gap

I identified in existing works was less uncommon, but just as important: my sexuality.

Queerly Ever After is a collection of short stories written for the bisexual girl who grew up uncertain, without words to describe her identity. It's for the bisexual teenager who did not have stories in which to explore her sexuality. It's for me, years ago. And for the me who is yet to come.

I wrote the first words of these stories in 2012, while I was still an undergraduate student—although, at the time, they were less 'stories' and more 'a collection of amorphous ideas and intent with no narrative structure'. I'm not sure how many of those early scribblings made it into the final product, but the process of writing, reading, and rewriting *Queerly Ever After* became immensely cathartic for me. Rereading the stories again—years later—to inform this afterword is having a similar effect.

Queerly Ever After features somewhere between nine and 15 short stories, depending on how you count. Each of these is based on source material from the traditional European fairy tale canon (Canepa 1997: 9; Harries 2001: 14): the stories of Charles Perrault, the Brothers Grimm, and Hans Christian Andersen. Familiar fables like *Snow White, The Ugly Duckling, Sleeping Beauty, Little Red Riding Hood*, and *Puss in Boots*.

I remember justifying the stories I chose to reimagine in my thesis by discussing the 'Western cultural context in which I reside' and the wide-reaching influence these particular tales had on children like me. Although it's true that these stories are perfect for reimagining simply because their familiarity and popularity mean they have perpetuated dominant heteropatriarchal discourse throughout Western society (Zipes 1987: 6-7; Lieberman 1972: 186), it would be disingenuous to say that was the main reason I selected these specific stories. I just really liked them.

I liked their narrative structures, their characters, the lessons they were trying to teach, and the gaps between their heteropatriarchal themes that inspired my queer imagination. It felt easy to imagine that the true reason Cinderella was ostracised all along was that she was queer, and it was magical to envision her running away with a princess instead of a prince.

But 'queering' well-known stories is not as simple as replacing every prince with a princess, dusting off my hands, and declaring the institution of fairy tales fixed for LGBTQ+ children everywhere. I know from experience that there's more to being a queer woman than meeting another woman at a royal ball and riding off into the sunset together.

Queerly Ever After has stories about queer women dating men, women, and nonbinary folks. Sometimes they get married, sometimes they don't. Sometimes they were in relationships before the story began, sometimes they meet during the course of the narrative, and some of the stories feature no relationships at all. But all of these women are equally valid and equally queer.

When I first started working on this collection, some people struggled to understand how I could represent plurisexuality—being attracted to multiple genders—without promiscuous characters or polyamorous relationships. If a woman marries a man, isn't she straight? If a woman isn't in a relationship, does she have a sexuality at all?

I remember presenting an early draft of my fairy tales to a senior academic at my university. He was confused and concerned. His argument was that fairy tales are for *children* and sex is not, and therefore sexuality should not be in fairy tales because there is simply no target audience for these stories.

Well, firstly, nobody tell him about the ridiculous number of *extremely* graphic queer fairy tale collections I still own from when I was researching the topic. But secondly—and more importantly—sexuality is not synonymous with sex. No matter where I am, who I'm with, and what I'm doing, I'm still a queer woman. My goal was to create a collection of fairy tales that showed how sexuality exists outside of relationships, assumptions, and visible behaviours.

Self-identification is extremely important for the queer community, so I reflected this by prioritising it in *Queerly Ever After*. Orndorff (1999) believes that it is important for members of the queer community to define their own sexuality; queer individuals cannot be categorised by others based on their relationships or behaviour, or even past attractions, particularly because identities can change over time (Ochs 2009). The only accurate way to learn a person's sexual identity is for them to define themselves (Eisner 2013: 20).

Although *Queerly Ever After* is not specifically designed for children, the stories incorporate queer perspectives without excluding this audience with references to sex, violence, abuse, and other themes that are better suited to the explicit collections hidden at the back of my bookshelf. Fairy tales are already a space where children explore their identities—including their sexual identities and their understanding of gender, sexuality, and sex or gender roles (Cranny-Francis 1992: 74-5; Curatolo 2012: 3; Zipes 1999: 75)—and I chose to add to that space, rather than make a new one.

The patriarchal gender roles traditionally taught in fairy tales (Zipes 1987: xi) are exclusionary and damaging to those who don't fit into binary and heteropatriarchal understandings of gender, attraction, and relationships (Baker 2010: 83; Neikirk 2009: 41). As such, queering fairy tales means complicating their relationship with gender and gender roles too.

One lesson taught by the European fairy tale canon is that boys can be active participants in the world while girls should remain passive. Girls are limited to the private sphere (Bacchilega 1997: 59), acting as a 'trophy' or 'object of exchange' (Baker 2010: 80). For example, in 'The Sleeping Beauty in the Wood' (Perrault 1969d), 'Briar Rose' (Grimm & Grimm 2013a), and 'Little Snow-White' (Grimm & Grimm 2013f), a prince rescues each protagonist from unconsciousness, which is the ultimate representation of passivity. In each of these stories, the prince is rewarded for his actions with marriage to the princess, with the princess acting as a 'trophy' or prize (Baker 2010: 80).

In *Queerly Ever After*, 'Amber' rejects the conclusion of its source material—'Little Snow-White'—with the eponymous character deciding to stay with the dwarfs rather than leave with the prince. When the prince arrives and sees Amber's inanimate body in her coffin, he says, 'I want to take her to my castle and encase her in glass so that her red lips can bring me happiness each time I look at them'. When Amber awakes, she refuses to accept this life and fulfil her gender role, in favour of empowering herself.

Amber's involvement in deciding whether she wants to marry the prince also subverts fairy tale conventions. When instructed to go to a prince's kingdom or marry a prince, it is typically assumed that a woman will comply without question, and her verbal consent is rarely included in the tale. This is seen in 'Rapunzel', where heteropatriarchal gender roles are reinforced as the prince 'led [Rapunzel] to his kingdom' (Grimm & Grimm 2013g: 83), an act that positions the prince as the 'leader' and Rapunzel as the 'follower'.

To subvert this narrative trajectory in 'Violet', the eponymous character and Amir have equal roles in the development of their relationship, which takes time to arise. After discovering Amir's presence in the shadows, Violet says, 'I shall not forgive a man who knows so much of me and yet of whom I know so little.' It takes many visits before Violet expresses her wish to go with Amir to the palace, a decision that the pair reach mutually. This man–woman relationship was included in the collection specifically to demonstrate their equal standing within their relationship, and to contrast this with the conventional model of marriage within the European fairy tale canon.

Queerly Ever After has also altered traditional fairy tale marriages by including weddings (or proposals) between pairings that are not man–woman. For example, in 'Crystal', Lua proposes to the eponymous character: 'Lua knelt, this time clutching a ring in place of a shoe. "Crystal, would you be my wife?" "I would be honoured," I replied. We kissed to a cacophony of echoing applause'.

These changes to the conventional structure of fairy tales may seem small, but they show their readers that the heteronormative and passive relationships of the traditional fairy tale canon are not their only option. Fairy tales have a significant influence over their audience and play a role in the socialisation of our children.

The fairy tale genre was modified in the eighteenth century, with the European canon taking on the dual purpose of entertaining and educating children (Bacchilega 1997: 2). The Brothers Grimm attempted to write tales that taught children how to behave in society, which was a mission continued and completed by Hans Christian Andersen when he wrote his canon (Zipes 1999: 80). Children still learn dominant social codes through fairy tales today (Zipes 2006: 1). Fairy tales allow children to explore what is considered 'moral behaviour' (Bettelheim 1975: 5) and the influence of these lessons leads Zipes (2006: 1) to believe that fairy tales are 'the most important cultural and social event in most children's lives'.

So what does it tell these children when they are told boys can be active but women should be passive? How does it affect their understanding of the world when the only 'happily ever after' they see is one where a man and a woman get married?

My research found other conventions of the fairy

tale canon that teach some questionable lessons to children too. Characters in fairy tales generally don't share their stories with their own voice, instead having those experiences retold by an external and impersonal narrator (Bacchilega 1997: 34).

The narrators of the traditional fairy tale canon use indirect speech, omniscience, and framing devices to separate themselves from the stories they tell. These narrators speak on behalf of characters, disempowering them and silencing them (Bacchilega 1997: 35). Sometimes this disempowerment happens in relatively harmless scenarios—such as when the narrator of 'Cinderella' says 'she thanked him very much' rather than including Cinderella's exact words (Grimm & Grimm 2013b: 115). However, sometimes this narrative technique has more problematic implications. For example, in 'Little Snow-White' the narrator speaks on behalf of the pre-adolescent Snow-White and claims she consents to travelling back to the prince's castle, but the reader never actually gets to see her speak.

I used direct attribution in each of my third-person tales, allowing my characters to speak for themselves. But—to take that even further—the majority of the tales in *Queerly Ever After* are written in first-person, which grants characters the agency to narrate their own stories. In 'Amber', the perspective shifts between multiple characters to ensure everyone is given the opportunity to share their experiences in their own words.

In addition to telling their own stories, each of my protagonists has their own name. The traditional fairy tale canon tends to disempower characters by giving them names based on their physical appearance (Snow White), clothes (Little Red Riding Hood), actions (Cinderella), status (Princess), or relationships (Sister) (Bettelheim 1975: 40)., Names are thematically relevant in many of the stories in *Queerly Ever After*, with several characters claiming their names or renaming themselves as an indicator of empowerment and agency.

The troll's narrative weaves its way throughout the entire collection, and focuses on the loss of her name and her search for a new one. The troll is referred to as 'a woman with no name' by Sterling in 'Silver' and a flashback to the troll first encountering the name 'troll' is included in 'Guilt'. In 'Violet', the troll says, 'I lost my name many years ago, beneath a bridge in another world. I hadn't any need for it anymore, so I tossed it in the river.'

The troll is one of the only characters in *Queerly Ever After* without a name, and is also the only character who acts as an omniscient narrator, as her story frames the many others in the collection. Her adherence to conventions of the fairy tale canon such as omniscience and framing are strange in their contrast to the other stories, and contribute to her feeling other-worldly.

But the troll is not emotionally detached in her omniscience. For example, in 'Innocence', the troll says, 'If I had looked up through the jagged frame in the workshop ceiling, I would have seen the pastel speck of the someone shrouded by grey clouds and white lightning. Contrary to the rules of your world, however, I needn't see the someone to know that she flew higher.' This scene reveals that the troll knows more than she would if the story was written with limited narration, but the technique of omniscience is destabilised by incorporating first- and second-person perspectives.

The jagged frame in the ceiling of the workshop is an explicit symbol in the text, but *Queerly Ever After* is equally preoccupied by frame stories as a narrative device. In both cases, frames change the way a narrative or parts of a narrative are perceived, either by limiting or expanding what the reader is able to see. Limiting what the reader—or a character—can see within a text can lead to or symbolise that agent's oppression; similarly, expanding their perception can liberate them (Bacchilega 1997: 35-6).

The short stories in the European fairy tale canon are sometimes referred to as compact tales, especially when compared to the less popular complex stories that were written by marginalised writers—both during the same period and in contemporary times (Harries 2001: 106). Within the compact tales of the European fairy tale canon, structural framing techniques are common, such as the repeated use of phrases like 'once upon a time' and 'happily ever after' (Harries 2001: 104; Orme 2010: 120).

These structural frames achieve one purpose: to inform the reader that they are entering a fairy tale setting, and therefore encouraging them to expect particular conventions and motifs (Harries 2001: 104; Orme 2010: 120). Starting a story with 'Once upon a time' is a particularly recognisable convention of the European fairy tale canon, so it can be jarring when placed within reimaginings that challenge fairy tale tropes (Lester 2007: 57).

Queerly Ever After uses the conventional phrase, but introduces it in longer, more complicated frame narratives.

Compact tales are typically only linked to one another by being published within one collection, with each tale featuring its own structural frames; however, the frames within complex tales serve a multitude of additional purposes. Detailed frame narratives and embedded tales with complex relationships to one another are used in progressive fairy tales to 'string various tales along like beads', influencing one another and allowing the reader to form a multiplicity of interpretations by examining how each story fits within the collection's larger context (Harries 2001: 106-7).

Harries (2001) explains some of the ways frame narratives and embedded tales traditionally interact with one another. A particularly simple model may feature a main tale within a contextualising frame narrative, and may contain one (or more) short embedded tales. However, a more complex model sees several tales connected to one another by a continuing frame narrative, with these main stories also featuring embedded tales of their own.

The frame structure of *Queerly Ever After* resembles the complex model offered by Harries (2001: 106-107), but with a few notable differences and additions. When I first started arranging and rearranging my stories, I moved index cards around on the carpet. Once I had my final structure, I turned it into a diagram that borrowed from Harries' format. The diagram represented each of the titled tales within the collection using one of three story types, which are based on Harries' models: the continuing frame, the main tales, and the embedded tales.

I used this diagram to figure out that *Queerly Ever After* has one continuing frame that is revisited three times, nine main tales—one of which is split in two—and two embedded tales. In addition to these, several other untitled embedded tales can be found throughout the collection, such as the flashbacks or fantasies of the eponymous character in 'Sterling', the stories Coral shares with Chelle in 'Coral', and the additional narrative Prince Alder recalls in 'Hazel'. Each embedded tale is denoted within the collection through formatting, including a deeper indentation.

Each frame in *Queerly Ever After* 'lend[s] authority and authenticity to the embedded tales' and provides context that allows the reader to understand 'why the embedded tales are important or suggests how they might be read' (Orme 2010: 121). These contexts add characterisation to the narrators and significance to their contents, further challenging the depersonalised conventional narrators of the European fairy tale canon.

In addition to creating intertextual 'stories resting within stories', complex tales also create intratextual links between tales within the same collection, which encourages the reader to see these stories in conversation with one another (Harries 2001: 18). The connections between the main tales in *Queerly Ever After* are important for adding to the complexity and multiplicity within the collection, as representations of multiplicity invite queer readings (Orme 2010: 117) and are indicative of the complexity of queer identities.

There are many ways to be a queer woman. I tend to use 'queer' to describe our community instead of LGBTQIA+ because that initialism is getting longer and doesn't include all the different identities that are out there. And there are a multitude of identities *within* each label. I label myself as 'bisexual' (primarily because most people have heard of it so it's easy to explain) but there is so much variation between each bisexual woman, just as there is between brunettes or people who wear glasses. The variation between each protagonist in *Queerly Ever After*, and the way their stories intersect with each other, was designed to convey some of these unique identities.

In addition to reading and researching fairy tales, I looked at coming-out stories as part of my thesis. *Queerly Ever After*'s stories are not explicitly coming out stories, but some of them do involve coming out narrative arcs. Coming-out stories are also interesting because they were the first texts to explicitly contain queer characters for the purpose of representing the identities and experiences of the queer community, allowing queer people to have authority over their own stories and influence non-queer audiences (Saxey 2008: 38). But they tend to tell a very specific queer story.

Coming-out stories are extremely conscious of their dual audience: they are written for other queer people, but they're also written for a heteropatriarchal society that might not understand what it's like to be queer. They were a way for queer audiences to put a (rainbow) flag in the sand and say, 'Hey, this is me, this is real, and you can't change me.' But this doesn't leave much room for variation in the types of stories being told, with queer writers prioritising a unified message over ambiguity, uncertainty, or multiplicity.

The first coming-out stories explored the identities of gay men, with lesbian anthologies of coming-out stories becoming an evolution of this genre as social change occurred around the acceptance of the gay and lesbian movement (Saxey 2008: 35, 77). This means that the conventions of the coming-out story formed around monosexual understandings of queerness, and can therefore be exclusionary of plurisexual identities (Saxey 2008: 134)—as well as other sexualities and genders (Zimman 2009).

Coming-out stories typically adhere to the four key conventions identified by Saxey (2008: 118-31), where queer characters must neglect the 'nuclear family' model, abandon life in small towns and communities, announce their sexuality, and renounce any attraction to genders other than their own. The last of these conventions is seen as pivotal to the coming-out story genre, but by definition it excludes queer folks who cannot renounce their attraction because they are attracted to more than one gender (Saxey 2008: 133). My coming-out story does not include me standing on a rooftop and shouting, 'I'm not attracted to men!' but it doesn't make my story any less valid.

Queerly Ever After uses intratextual connections to explore the multiplicity of queer stories. The collection forms links between characters who are ostracised from their families, characters who choose to leave their communities, and characters who feel accepted and supported where they are.

Teale and Violet were once attracted to one another, leading to Violet being abandoned in a tower by her father; there's a reference to the 'wild ducks' from 'Teale' in 'Sienna'; Violet and Amir's children— Sol and Lua—are the prince and princess in 'Crystal'; Tabby and Olive are sisters, with Olive still living in their kingdom and Tabby having run away at sixteen; and Prince Alder in 'Hazel' was a descendent of the troll in 'Tabby'.

More connections can be found between the continuing frame and main tales. In addition to 'Innocence', 'Guilt', and 'Clemency', the characters from the continuing frame appear in a number of other tales. The troll appears in 'Violet', where she tells the tale of 'Sienna', she is referenced in 'Tabby', and appears in 'Coral', where she tells the tale of 'Hazel'. The troll's narrative arc chronologically differing from that of the reader's further emphasises the ambiguous and mysterious nature of the troll, revealing the way she travels through time and has lived for many human lifetimes, even as only one season has passed for Innocence. The troll's chronology makes each of these tales seem as though they are both connected within one universe and disconnected across worlds, while connections between the main tales close the distance between the protagonists and their experiences.

Just as the troll's narrative frames are used to limit what can be seen by characters and the reader, mirrors are also a form of frame that presents a particular image or reflection to that same audience (Bacchilega 1997: 10). Also similar to frames, mirrors can exist as both symbols and narrative devices within a story (Schanoes 2009: 5), or even as reflections of a storyteller's ideologies.

As Jackson (2013: 87) notes, in fantasy the mirror is used as a way of creating distance between a person and the 'self' as others perceive it. They are able to position the self as an 'object' (Jackson 2013: 88), and therefore have potential to reveal oppression. Mirrors are able to reflect oppressive perspectives, or allow characters to see their reflection and identity in new ways (Bacchilega 1997: 35-6). The ways that mirrors explore identity and expose oppression have led to them becoming a key motif and symbol within the feminist fairy tales subgenre.

Mirrors are used in the European fairy tale canon to represent the heteropatriarchal male gaze, and act as symbols for the oppression of women and minority groups (Bacchilega 1997: 34; Schanoes 2009: 6). For example, in 'Little Snow-White' (Grimm & Grimm 2013f) the magic mirror encourages the stepmother to compete with other women and judge her own self-worth based on her appearance (Bacchilega 1997: 34).

Mirrors and reflections feature in every tale within *Queerly Ever After*, and are used to expose the oppression faced by plurisexual protagonists and other characters, as well as being reclaimed symbols used to frame characters' identities. The most significant mirror in the collection is found in the cathedral in 'Innocence'. This mirror is imposing—within the scene, and within the collection—as the shattered pieces of this reflection allow Innocence and the troll to move through worlds and experience the other tales within *Queerly Ever After*. As the 'fierce wind ripped doorways between the worlds', Innocence is able to 'see herself reflected in the infinite colours of the kaleidoscope, the colours of worlds she did not recognise and faces that somehow resembled hers'—the faces of the other protagonists in the collection.

However, the pieces of the wicked mirror do more than simply reflect the faces of the protagonist back to Innocence and the troll; they are also intended to be markers of the wickedness of people who ostracise and oppress queer characters throughout the collection. The pieces of mirror find their way into other worlds and corrupt people's perspectives:

Some ... fragments were large enough that they might be found and formed into window panes or spectacles through which the world could seem distorted and broken, when looked through by those with weak hearts and cold eyes. Other shards were so small that they could be inhaled, lodging themselves within a person's throat and colouring their words with hidden hatred.

This motif borrows from Andersen's (2013c) 'The Snow Queen', which features a mirror that distorts the landscapes it reflects; this mirror is also shattered into 'a hundred million million and more' pieces, which then 'flew about', becoming stuck in people's eyes and hearts, or were made into window panes and spectacles (Andersen 2013c: 316).

The pieces of the Snow Queen's mirror in *Queerly Ever After* reveal themselves in the cat's eyes when it examines Cloud and in Violet's father's eyes angry when he abandons her in the tower he built her. They're in Sienna's throat when she impersonates the offensive wolf and in Pearl's when screeches in 'Crystal'. The king demands Hyla leaves the palace with 'his eyes shimmering with cold glass' and the teacher looks through 'the distorted glass of the schoolroom windows' when she chastises Ivory for being attracted to girls. Pieces of the wicked mirror in the eyes and throats of these characters connect them, both to each other and to the oppression they perpetrate.

But these shards of mirror also suggest that discrimination and intolerance are not a default state. These characters are not naturally cruel; rather, these beliefs are introduced to them. In the case of *Queerly Ever After*, the influence is a magical mirror; in real life, it's socialisation and miseducation.

Mirrors are also reclaimed by protagonists in *Queerly Ever After* as positive symbols of their identities, like slurs and insults are reclaimed by the queer community to unite and empower them. In 'Teale', as the eponymous character rises from the river, she 'dash[es] her reflection'. This is symbolic of her casting aside her previous identity as she begins a journey that might help her find acceptance for who she is. In 'Amber', the eponymous character says that she 'preferred to admire [her] mud-streaked cheeks in the uncertain reflections of the river' rather than in mirrors. Rivers can represent movement, pathways, and freedom, so it's fitting that queer protagonists find more comfort in reflective water than reflective glass.

In addition to featuring within the stories, mirrors feature in the overall structure of the collection as well. The tales that comprise *Queerly Ever After* are designed so the two halves of the collection are reflections of one another. 'Guilt' is the eighth tale of the collection and is at the centre of the structure, with seven tales before it and seven tales after it. The frame narratives 'Innocence' and 'Clemency' are positioned as tale one and tale 15, reflections of one another. 'Teale' and 'Ivory' are tales two and 14, and both focus on non-romantic relationships; the only other tales that do not feature romantic relationships are tales 7 and 9, which are two halves of the same narrative and sit on either side of the central revisiting of the continuing frame narrative.

'Amber' and 'Olive' are the two main tales with nonbinary main characters, and these are tales three and 13. 'Violet' and 'Coral' are the two main tales that contain titled embedded tales and sit opposite one another. Tales six and 10 — 'Crystal' and 'Tabby'—are also reflections, with Crystal becoming a princess while Tabby abandons her life of royalty.

The possibility of tales being mirrors of one another is suggested within the tales themselves, particularly in Innocence's thoughts about the worlds she visits. In 'Silver', Innocence refers to the world and says it 'could be a reflection of the one I left'. She also reveals that the stories and characters within the collection reflect one another in 'Clemency', when she describes the 'women who stood before me like mirrors, both of the person I am and the person I inhabited'.

Smolkin and Young (2011: 217) describe stories as having the potential to be 'self-affirming' mirrors for children who are able to see a reflection of their own culture or identity in the narratives they read and characters they meet. But how do fairy tales reflect these identities when they tell and retell the same heteropatriarchal stories over and over again?

Queerly Ever After holds a fractured mirror to the fairy tale genre, distorting its reflection so it can 'multiply its refractions and expose its artifices' (Bacchilega 1997: 23). By introducing differences and challenging genre conventions, I hoped to expose and question the tropes that we all accept as a necessary part of the fairy tale genre (Bacchilega 1997: 36, 50).

I love fairy tales. After reading many pages of me criticising them for their heteropatriarchal morals, I'll forgive you if that comes as a surprise. But, as much as I love fairy tales, I've always seen myself more in *Sleeping Beauty*'s evil fairy godmother and the wicked swamp witch in *Hansel and Grethel*, rather than in any of the princesses. I'm opinionated, I'm independent, and I don't know anybody who would dream of calling me passive.

But I deserve to be a princess too—not just the monstrous queer villain who has been shunned from society. So, I wrote some stories where women like me get to be the main character, in the hope that maybe they help other young girls imagine themselves dancing in ball gowns, running through villages, and saving themselves from towers.

And maybe, after all that, they will still prefer to see themselves as witches and trolls, living in the dirt beneath bridges and in forests. That's fine too.

*

I put down my pen.

Innocence turns to me, an eyebrow raised. 'Is that it? Are you... finished?'

I laugh. 'Yes, and no. Is my work ever truly finished?'

We pause, the dust motes dancing between us in the light. I close the distance, and Innocence smiles.

'So, what's next?

References

European fairy tale canon

Andersen, HC 2013a, 'The Little Match Girl', in *The Complete Illustrated Works of Hans Christian Andersen*, Bounty Books, London, pp. 357-58.

—— 2013b, 'The Little Sea Maid', in *The Complete Illustrated Works of Hans Christian Andersen*, Bounty Books, London, pp. 543-59.

—— 2013c, 'The Snow Queen', in *The Complete Illustrated Works of Hans Christian Andersen*, Bounty Books, London, pp. 315-40.

—— 2013d, 'The Ugly Duckling', in *The Complete Illustrated Works of Hans Christian Andersen*, Bounty Books, London, pp. 155-67.

Grimm, J & Grimm, W 2013a, 'Briar Rose', in *The Complete Illustrated Works of the Brothers Grimm*, Bounty Books, London, pp. 236-41.

—— 2013b, 'Cinderella', in *The Complete Illustrated Works of the Brothers Grimm*, Bounty Books, London, pp. 114-21.

—— 2013c, 'The Frog Prince', in *The Complete Illustrated Works of the Brothers Grimm*, Bounty Books, London, pp. 1-4.

—— 2013d, 'Hansel and Grethel', in *The Complete Illustrated Works of the Brothers Grimm*,

Bounty Books, London, pp. 66-72.

—— 2013e, 'Little Red-Cap', in *The Complete Illustrated Works of the Brothers Grimm*, Bounty Books, London, pp. 107-10.

—— 2013f, 'Little Snow-White', in *The Complete Illustrated Works of the Brothers Grimm*, Bounty Books, London, pp. 250-9.

—— 2013g, 'Rapunzel', in *The Complete Illustrated Works of the Brothers Grimm*, Bounty Books, London, pp. 77-82.

Perrault, C 1969a, 'Cinderella or the Little Glass Slipper', in *Perrault's Fairy Tales*, Dover Publications, New York, pp. 65-78.

—— 1969b, 'Little Red Riding Hood', in *Perrault's Fairy Tales*, Dover Publications, New York, pp. 23-30.

—— 1969c, 'The Master Cat or Puss in Boots', in *Perrault's Fairy Tales*, Dover Publications, New York, pp. 45-58.

—— 1969d, 'The Sleeping Beauty in the Wood', in *Perrault's Fairy Tales*, Dover Publications, New York, pp. 1-22.

Other sources

Bacchilega, C 1997, *Postmodern Fairy Tales: Gender and Narrative* Strategies, University of Pennsylvania Press, Philadelphia.

Baker, DJ 2010, 'Monstrous Fairytales: Towards an Ecriture Queer', *Colloquy: Text, Theory, Critique*, vol. 20, pp. 79-103.

Bettelheim, B 1975, *The Uses of Enchantment: The Meaning and Importance of Fairy Tales*, Vintage, New York.

Canepa, NL 1997, *Out of the Woods: The Origins of the Literary Fairy Tale in Italy and France*, Wayne State University Press, Detroit.

Cranny-Francis, A 1992, *Engendered Fiction: Analysing Gender in the Production and Reception of Texts*, New South Wales University Press, Kensington, Australia.

Curatolo, B 2012, 'Queering "Happily Ever After": Queer Narratives Expose Heteronormalcy in Fairy Tales', *Senior Honors Projects*. vol. 3, <http://collected.jcu.edu/honorspapers/3>.

Eisner, S 2013, *Bi: Notes for a Bisexual Revolution*, Seal Press, New York.

Gamble, S 2008, 'Penetrating to the Heart of the Bloody Chamber: Angela Carter and the Fairy Tale', in S Benson (ed.), *Contemporary Fiction and the Fairy Tale*, Wayne State University Press, Detroit, pp. 20-46.

Harries, EW 2001, *Twice Upon a Time: Women Writers and the History of the Fairy Tale*, Princeton

University Press, Princeton.

Jackson, R 2013, *Fantasy*, Routledge, Abingdon, UK.

Lester, NA 2007, '(Un) Happily Ever After: Fairy Tale Morals, Moralities, and Heterosexism in Children's Texts', *Journal of Gay & Lesbian Issues in Education*, vol. 4, no. 2, pp. 55-74.

Lieberman, MR 1972, 'Some Day My Prince Will Come: Female Acculturation Through the Fairy Tale', *College English*, vol. 34, no. 3, pp. 383-95.

Ochs, R 2009, *Getting Bi: Voices of Bisexuals around the World*, Bisexual Resource Center, Boston, Massachusetts.

Orme, J 2010, 'Mouth to Mouth: Queer Desires in Emma Donoghue's Kissing the Witch', *Marvels & Tales*, vol. 24, no. 1, pp. 116-30.

Orndorff, K 1999, *Bi Lives: Bisexual Women Tell Their Stories*, See Sharp Press, Tucson, Arizona.

Propp, V 1968, *Morphology of the Folk Tale*, University of Texas Press, Austin, Texas.

Saxey, E 2008, *Homoplot: The Coming out Story and Gay, Lesbian and Bisexual Activity*, Peter Lang Publishing, New York.

Schanoes, VL 2009, 'Book as Mirror, Mirror as Book: The Significance of the Looking-Glass in Contemporary Revisions of Fairy Tales', *Journal of the Fantastic in the Arts*, vol. 20, no. 1, pp. 5-23.

Smolkin, LB & Young, CA 2011, 'Missing Mirrors, Missing Windows: Children's Literature

Textbooks and LGBT Topics', *Language Arts*, vol. 88, no. 3, pp. 217-25.

Zipes, J 1987, *Don't Bet on the Prince: Contemporary Feminist Fairy Tales in North America and England*, Routledge, New York.

—— 2006, *Fairytales and the Art of Subversion*, Routledge, New York.

—— 1999, *When Dreams Came True: Classical Fairy Tales and Their Tradition*, Routledge, New York.

www.ingramcontent.com/pod-product-compliance
Lightning Source LLC
Chambersburg PA
CBHW020152120726
47903CB00007B/2521